First published in Great Britain in 2011 by Comma Press
www.commapress.co.uk

First published in Prague as *O Létajících Objektech* by Argo, 2004.

The moral rights of Emil Hakl (aka Jan Beneš) to be identified as the Author
of this Work, and of Petr Kopet and Karen Reppin to be identified as the
Translators of this Work, have been asserted in accordance with the Copyright
Designs and Patents Act 1988.

A CIP catalogue record of this book is available from the British Library.

This collection is entirely a work of fiction. The characters and incidents
portrayed in it are entirely the work of the author's imagination. The opinions of
the author are not those of the publisher.

ISBN    1905583389
ISBN-13    978 1905583386

**LOTTERY FUNDED**

The publisher gratefully acknowledges assistance from the Arts Council England
North West. With the support of the Culture Programme (2007-2013) of the
European Union.

Education and Culture DG

**Culture Programme**

Culture

This project has been funded with support from the European Commission. This
publication reflects the views only of the author, and the Commission cannot be
held responsible for any use which may be made of the information contained
therein. This project was subsidised by the Ministry of Culture of the Czech
Republic.

**MINISTRY OF CULTURE
CZECH REPUBLIC**

Set in Bembo 11/13 by David Eckersall
Printed and bound in England by Short Run Press.

# ON FLYING OBJECTS

by
Emil Hakl

Translated by
Petr Kopet & Karen Reppin

# Contents

*To experience bizarre ambience, one doesn't need to take part in the exhumation of a murdered body in a remote forest clearing on a stormy night. A harmless get-together with casual evening companions may provide just as strong a feeling of horror.*

Alfred Kubin, 1933

# Close Encounters

ON SUNDAY NIGHT, due to a conjunction of uninteresting circumstances, I found myself at the intersection of Vinohradská and Jičínská streets. I stood there looking up at the humongous, square UFO that had recently landed there, known as Flóra Palace. A thin white beam cut straight up through the smoky sky above its roof. Although it was past 10pm, it was bustling inside. Lively, gesturing little figures floated by on the escalators. Shops were blasting out noise. Cafés were buzzing. Young shopkeeper girls, trapped by way of 'help wanted', were yawning. Hundreds of mandibles were processing salads, potato chips, sandwiches; pedipalps smeared with lipstick were sucking in spaghetti; and the broken chelicerae of old geezers were grinding away at chicken schnitzels. Before the entrance, an unfinished fountain gurgled among piles of black marble slabs.

I realized I was hungry – my last meal that day had been my breakfast – and I headed for the brightly lit entrance. On the ground floor I got myself half a grilled chicken, on the first a new jacket, on the second the soundtrack to *Lost Highway,* and on the third a nifty lighter. After that I made my way among bare-bellied chicks and red-striped little shavers and all sorts of slick, phoney imbeciles and super awkward hip-hoppers under the building's roof. There was a multiplex. Without much thinking, I purchased a ticket. I checked the show time. I still had twenty minutes. I hid myself in a bistro behind an artificial palm tree and ordered a cup of joe. A dolled-up, restless dude with a petite, misty-eyed babe sat not far from me. She was squeezing her black-clad little tush against him under the table. Which he was oblivious to since he was busy with the collection of rings on his hand, sliding them off and back on in different combinations.

'I'll go completely nuts if you don't go there,' she told him in Slovak in her dim sugar-sweet little voice.

'I will for ffffuck's sake, I told ya I will, told ya I don't wanna hear about it right now!'

'I'll go nuts for sure if you don't go,' she continued.

'Told ya I'll go, don't believe me or what?' he was whispering and fuming.

'Nobody does.'

'Nobody does, so what's the fuss,' he suddenly started to laugh and downed his drink.

His girlie started to cough.

'Koochy-koo,' he babbled and gently stroked her hair, 'Have more booze, that'll do ya good…'

She shook her head and pressed herself against him again.

In a few minutes I was sitting in a spacious, new-smelling theatre. The film started. It was called *Pupendo*. There was popcorn crackling and coke swooshing all around. I tore a leg off my chicken in the dark, took a bite and watched the screen with the new jacket on my lap. I found myself laughing. Everyone around me was laughing too. 'Dude, Jarda Dušek is ace, dude!' someone spluttered at the back of my neck. I returned the picked-clean bone to the bag and looked around. The audience was rolling with laughter.

I twisted off a wing and started to pick the meat off.

Next morning I discovered that the display of my Siemens mobile phone had turned black overnight. I madly pushed the buttons but to no avail; the display looked like the entrance to a tunnel. The phone was still under warranty, so I picked myself up and went to a T-Mobile centre on

Londýnská Street. A flawless, blue-eyed, young thing was standing behind the counter. A white bra under a white shirt. I explained my problem to her.

'Yes, but this is mechanical damage. That's not covered by the warranty.'

'But I'm sure there hasn't been any mechanical impact to it,' I objected, 'and the mobile was still working fine last night – this only happened today.'

'This is mechanical damage, and that's not covered under the warranty,' she repeated.

'How can this be mechanical damage when there's not even a scratch on the outside?' I asked.

'It's mechanical damage, which is not covered under the warranty,' she answered and used that line several more times in our exchange.

'It was not mechanically damaged because I never slammed into anything,' I kept telling her.

'That's what you are telling us, but *we* are telling *you* that it's mechanical damage,' she concluded.

For a moment it dawned on me that I was in the middle of a game without being able to learn, at least approximately, what the rules are. And then there was this foul copper taste in my mouth. A short-circuit. The wiring. Dust burnt in semiconductors. Viscous walls you could stick an arm into all the way to the elbow. Swaying floors. Disappearing and reappearing rooms where things are happening. Definitely an out-of-whack balance between the acid and alkaline.

The lordly mouse was staring at me coldly. I suddenly felt she knew exactly what was going through my mind. That this is part of her daily routine. I gawked at her. She gazed back at me with porcelain indifference.

'All right then, why don't you put down a five-thousand-korun deposit, and we'll send it off to be repaired; it'll take at least three months though,' she said, showing some mercy by going strictly by the book.

I could feel the onset of paranoia in my gut. I felt that

I may soon engage in something that could be classified as a reason to call security, so instead I turned around, crossed the street, got into the subway and headed for the Siemens Centre in Dejvice.

'This is mechanical damage, and that's not covered by the warranty, but we can replace the display for three thousand, which will take eight weeks,' said a well-groomed twenty-eight year-old hunk whose likes and dislikes were written all over his face. Hockey. Vacationing in Spain. Cars. Jerks.

'You make me want to wretch,' I told him.

'You're entitled to that view,' he replied with a pleasant smile.

That was the end of our discussion.

On the subway train there was a man on the opposite seat absorbed in a book called *Questions and Answers*. He would read a bit, frown, look up, then turn the book upside down, read a bit again, raise his eyebrows with satisfaction, turn it again, read another sentence and frown again.

There's a small mobile phone shop on my street. I pushed the door open and headed in, hoping to be able to vent about my woes a bit. The salesman was leaning against the counter and sweating. 'Uh-oh!' he said in welcome, 'the display needs replacing.'

'I know,' I sighed.

'This will set you back at least eight hundred if not more!' he continued, 'and it won't be done right away either.'

'Then when?' I asked.

'The earliest... Really the earliest would be the day after tomorrow...' he answered.

I gave him the device and a thousand korun even though he never asked for a down payment, and went for a walk. I had my new jacket on, which glowed in a beautifully grey-green autumn colour with a touch of blue. I put my hands in the pockets. One of them felt something. I pulled out a pack of round stickers. There were five, and they all read: *I love Pupendo!*[1] Don't know how they got there. I looked around, spotted a polished, fancy gas–guzzler and attached them all to its windshield.

When I was crossing Bezruč Park, building and factory sirens started to whine all across the Prague Basin. Two mothball noblewomen clicking their municipal heels a little ahead of me stopped and looked around indignantly.

'They must be testing sirens,' stated one and straightened her soft, puffy poke bonnet as if the fate of the world depended on it. 'Or there's another anniversary of some sort,' said the other.

A young girl with her hair cut short and her face covered with reddish pimples was coming down the pavement, carrying a large black dog in her arms. The dog was wailing and licking her forearm. Her t-shirt was completely covered in blood. An arrow stuck out of a wound on the back of the dog's neck. Blood was dripping onto the pavement.

'Somebody shot my dog,' she said.

'Where?' I asked pointlessly.

'Just around the corner in the park... Can you call somebody?'

The dog was shaking and obviously on his way out.

'How did this happen?' I asked.

'I don't know,' said the girl, 'I don't know! I just heard a sort of a swish – I don't know! Can you call somebody?'

I took a few steps towards the intersection and flagged down a taxi. The guy behind the wheel drifted towards the pavement and looked at me inquiringly.

'To the vet,' I pointed to the bloodied girl with her dog.

'You can't be serious,' he replied, closed the door and drove off.

'Would you try pulling it out...?' it occurred to the girl. 'I'll hold him. Stay Bubánek, my dear, this gentleman will

1. Popular Czech comedy film set in the Soviet era, released in 2003.

help you...'

The arrow was short and thick with plastic fletchings at the end, most likely something that came from one of the tons of crossbows sold everywhere. Most of it was stuck in the wound. I tried touching it. The dog cried out in pain and the girl shrieked.

'This won't work,' I said.

The girl sat down on the curb. She lay the dog on the grass. The pooch was shaking and rasping. His left front and hind legs twitched as if he was trying to run away from it all. The girl kept stroking his head. 'Someone shot him,' she kept repeating. 'Someone shot him.'

I sat down on the curb beside them. While the girl was stroking the dog, it occurred to me that humans will, in the end, have to perform vivisection on themselves. But – it dawned on me as the dog's shaking quickened – it would need to be done without bias, which means with a measure of cynicism. Because if they derived satisfaction from it they'd either go bonkers or become arrogant, I thought.

In that instant the dog made a sound for which there is no word. Something between a desperate, almost human-like blurt and a futile attempt to speak. Then he died. The girl kept stroking him. I got up and started to walk away. After a few steps I turned around. The girl was looking at me. She was really quite ugly. She had bleached hair, her fair mousy roots showing.

'You're all sons of bitches,' she said quietly.

'I know,' I said.

# That's America

I REACHED THE only empty table and before I even had a chance to order, Mikeš, followed by Ivanka and some smallish woman with a mop of hair, showed up.

'Diz is Mrs. Shapiro from California,' Mikeš introduced her. 'En dis iz Honzík... what do they have on tab here?'

'Staropramen,' I answered and shook hands with the short woman. Her hand was firm and her handshake like a bricklayer's. The four of us spent the next hour conversing. Then Ivanka and Mikeš got up to go because they still had other plans with someone somewhere else, and the American said she was gonna have another beer with me since she didn't even have a chance to find out what and how I was doing.

'All right, we're splitting, and you folks have fun,' said Mikeš, and I felt his expression was somehow too serious; other times he'd crack a little joke or something.

I was left alone with her. Her face was thin, her grey eyes impenetrable, and her salt and pepper hair thick and wavy. I couldn't get enough of her hair. She had enough for three women and each would still have more than enough. The sound of the rain coming down in irregular gusts could be heard from outside. I had toothache. The jukebox was playing *Nightclubbing* the fourth time around.

'Do you like Iggy Pop?'

'Not really.'

'So what do you like?'

I named a few bands.

'I like Iggy Pop,' she responded.

I decided to speed things up a bit. 'And at the moment I'm not working, I sit at home day and night and read and watch TV.'

'Hm, but that's a little...' one could see her thinking about how strong a word to choose, 'a little stupid, no?'

'It is, but it relaxes me.'

'It relaxes you?'

'Sure. Because it's got nothing to do with reality. It's a world of its own.'

'And you don't mind doing nothing?'

'Well, I do feel a bit guilty, that's for sure.'

'So why don't you find something?'

'Because for at least once in my life I want to have a few years just to myself. Two or three.'

'And then?'

'Then I'll throw myself back into it and won't get out before I die.'

'So what do you watch on TV?'

'Doesn't matter, pretty much everything except for politics, most series, game shows and American movies.'

'I see. And why do you leave out American movies?'

'Because I don't like them at all.'

'Why?' her grey eyes were assessing me.

'Because they commonly use emotional blackmail of the worst kind.'

'Really?' she said and took a sip of her beer.

'Of course,' I answered and put my nose to my pint. I looked at her through the thick tempered glass; her forehead was frighteningly bulgy, her big bushy hair had a reddish tinge to it, and below all that was a strict, tiny little mouth. She looked dissatisfied.

'But what about *The Old Man and the Sea* with Spencer Tracy?' she pondered.

'That's the shittiest of them all!' I said and my heart began to throb. 'With that old fart speaking to a fish as if he was giving a lecture to all of humanity; and the whole thing is all sooo important! *The Old Man and the Sea* is an artificial, overstylized, schmaltzy, and absolutely phony piece of shit! It couldn't really be much better anyway, since the author of the book was pretty crappy to begin with. I'd rather go for a movie like *Robocop* which, if nothing else, is at least honest, and there's probably more truth to it than anybody suspects – we'll find out soon enough. But something that bugs me even in this one is your self-centered paranoia, USA versus the conspiring rest of the universe!'

'Maybe, but perhaps there are still some good American movies...'

'Yes, there are exceptions, but they're no big deal considering that Hollywood is nothing but a digital cultural concentration camp, plus there are film cultures in which a bad film tends to be the exception,' I said while feeling that my adrenalin was yet again doing me a disservice.

'Which ones for instance?'

I couldn't but carry on: 'German, Italian, Russian, Polish, Hungarian, as well as Dutch and Estonian and Finnish...'

I'd never seen an Estonian film. I'd seen about four Dutch films including a comedy in which people were constantly confusing a poodle with a broom, and a postman, who was actually a postwoman, with a hitman.

'All right,' she said through the thicket of her incredible hair. 'So you don't like Iggy Pop and you don't like American movies. So tell me, what *do* you like?'

What is it I like? Well, the rain pouring down on the roofs outside, the shining street-car tracks. Birds' singing at four in the morning. Those shaky stars there above the České Středohoří. Dung beetles thundering down the needle-covered ground. More and more the same friends. Soft blondes in bookkeeping offices. Pale girls from concrete suburban neighbourhoods. All those permanently pissed off rum-guzzling old farts. All those frog princes educated in humanities who are so good to gab with and who won't lift a finger for you later. And actually even all those wide boys who screw you before you even notice them simply because that's how they communicate. All those who make it a joy living on this planet populated with superstitions, hollow illusions and quiet, persistent manias. Fuck, all of it...! I like all of it! Everything that's here and will go on being here when I'm not around! All of it!

'All of it,' I said.

'What?'

'Well, Finnish vodka, for one, especially when the weather's crappy like this. You want one?'

'Absolutely.'

We tipped back our Finlandias and moved on to subjects more spiritual.

'So what about you? How do you feel about living this life?' I asked a question I could hardly answer myself.

'For me it's from one wall to the other; I'm a dancer, I have my own ballet school in California and I feel a little insecure 'cause I'm not so young anymore,' she said without thinking. 'You have good beer here, the service sucks, but the beer is good... Anyway, other than that I'm basically satisfied; it's just that lately I've been feeling kinda funny, something's missing but I'm not quite sure what. It's like something's been *lost*, how can I say... I have a husband and kids and work and a house, but something's missing. It may just be a small thing, like oxytocin–'

'What's oxytocin?'

'It's a chemical that gets released in the female brain during fucking. This chemical encourages the ability to socialize. The contrary situation leads to isolation, which is not pleasant; and that's why regularity in those matters is important.'

'I see,' I said. 'You know, for me nothing happens in my life for the longest time, and then boom! I'm in the thick of it day in and day out.'

'Hm... For the woman it's better if it's regular, even

once a month, rather than by fits and starts.'

I was alarmed. My life was actually based on irregularity. If she's right and if it's true in general, then I'll need to reevaluate from scratch everything that's ever happened to me.

I said that to her. She laughed for about five minutes.

'So how do you feel about living this life?' she continued after she'd finished laughing.

'I don't really know; it's like some kind of game, where the purpose is to get ahead; and you only get ahead by taking apart and abolishing everything that's no longer relevant. There are some pretty frightening figures roaming about, but they're there just to keep it interesting for you; the main stuff happens in empty space, where there are empty space suits floating around–'

'Excuse me?'

'Space suits,' I heard myself saying, after all I'd had quite a few vodkas by then. 'And when I get near one of them, I climb in and stay in it for a while. I try it out, see how it works, push this and that, I lounge around in it and socialize, I go to work somewhere in it. But then it starts to fall apart all on me and it's time to try something new.'

'But I don't think you're in a space suit right now,' she said cautiously.

'I certainly am.' I tugged at my face and pulled at my love-handles. 'Life happens only if you're inside a space suit, because outside the space suit there's nothing, absolutely nothing. Life is just a laugh... all around it's just a laugh,' I said in my intoxicated English but the 'laugh' which came out of my mouth most probably sounded more like 'love' to her.

'Yes!' she blurted out and sharply nipped my lower lip. 'Yes... You have... a beautiful manly mouth! Beautiful manly mouth!' She whispered to me in a deep voice while pulling me towards her. I tried to back away a little but she wouldn't let go. My lip was being stretched and becoming numb and then she passionately whispered in my ear, 'I've got my life, my husband, two kids, I've got work I love, I'm happy and satisfied... But today I wanna forget all this... Today it's just me and you, the two of us... And I don't care what happens tomorrow...'

She was squeezing my lower lip, gnawing at it and twisting it. I saw, in my peripheral vision, that everyone was watching us. I tried not to imagine what this must look like. Just the fact that not a single person smiled spoke for itself. It was as if, in part apathetic, in part disgusted, they were waiting to see what this would turn into – bodily harm or a spontaneous hysterical copulation or what. Legitimising our situation by publicly kissing her seemed to me the most feasible option. As soon as I thought of that she did it herself. I could feel her tongue fiddling all the way up to my tonsils. At the same time she kept making all kinds of statements. It was as if I were kissing a drunk employee of a funeral home.

Everyone went back to their conversations. Half an hour later we paid the bill and went out on to the wet éiûkov pavement. Walking down the hill we soon found ourselves in a gypsy neighbourhood full of flashing lights down by the Viktoria stadium; an anthill full of pawnshops, discount shops, video rental places, second-hand shops, laser-lit amusement arcades and bars.

One could hear the hoopla, mobile phones, dim electronic music, chatter, insults and laughter coming out of the colourful little caves. On the corner a hulking dark-haired woman was vomiting while her slick handsome dude in a beautiful shiny leather jacket lightened her burden:

'Get movin' cunt, we should've been there already. Told yer not to drink! I told yer!'

Meanwhile it started to drizzle again.

'This is the landscape of my childhood,' I said. 'This is where I grew up.'

'Really?' she responded.

'Yep. But back then it looked different around here; the soft and comfortable Middle Ages ruled, there were bats and owls flying through the night, you didn't have those watering holes and people did their laundry only on Friday and Saturday nights.'

'Hm... I grew up in a place where the only thing that changed since I was born was the church. It collapsed during an earthquake so they rebuilt it.'

While talking she pulled up her skirt, squatted and pissed right in the middle of the street. She wasn't bothered in the slightest by the dumbfounded Opel slowing down a few metres behind her.

'Watch for the car,' I said.

'That's all right, he'll wait,' she said undisturbed.

I watched the wild golden stream making its way among the cobblestones in the headlights and I must say I was quite taken by it. We couldn't have walked more than twenty metres when all of a sudden she pulled up her t-shirt.

'Look.' she said in a serious, deep voice. 'This is my American body, these are my American breasts... I'm normally quite modest, I hope you understand, but now you have the opportunity... now you can... you know.'

I did know quite clearly. I myself have been longing all my life for nothing but events that can be neither influenced, nor initiated or stopped; that come just like the earthquake that destroyed the church in her hometown. But she didn't choose a particularly suitable place. There were fluorescent lights buzzing above the entrance to some late night establishment not far from us. Cigarette lights quietly glowed on both sides of the entrance. I pulled her t-shirt back down. Mrs. Shapiro, however, was not about to give up so easily. Again she vigorously pulled up her top. And I pulled it back down again. This continued for some time.

Different comments came at us out of the darkness: 'Let her take it off!' 'Go home, buddy, get out of the way!' 'Leave her here and get lost!'

It was high time to take off. Even she understood that by now. I grabbed her hand and started pulling her away. After a few steps I could hear that we were being quietly followed by three or perhaps more of those guys. Clint Eastwood would perhaps choose a different strategy but I pushed her into the entrance of a éiûkov apartment building around the first corner, then dragged her into the courtyard and there behind a pile of mouldy rags and broken wardrobes began to rub her back comfortingly. The entrance door slammed. A dog barked on a landing above. Then silence. The short woman stood right next to me and her wet hair brushed over my chin as she breathed at my neck like a calf. So there, nitwit, I thought to myself, if what they're after is cracking your skull for kicks and raping this majorette, you couldn't have picked a better place for them.

'Don't worry,' said Shapiro in a very quiet voice. 'I'm calm.'

'Me, too,' I lied. 'But it can't hurt to wait here a bit.'

'Yes,' she whispered.

Several minutes passed. The smell of urine and rotting wood was slowly making its way to our hearts. We started to walk back to the entrance. I took the handle and opened the door. The street was empty. We went out and walked towards the stadium, which was quiet at night. The grey and green and bluish and yellowish apartment buildings stood on the hillside above the Viktoria, resembling a rock formation.

'So what now?' I said.

'The best thing would be to go to my place and have some hot tea.' Her teeth chattered from the cold.

'Where do you live?'

'Near this kind of a round square where there's nothing but grass and tram tracks.'

I tried to flag down a cab a couple of times to no avail. Finally a blasé fucker in his little shiny Ford pulled up.

'To Kulaťák,' I said.

The driver nodded and continued talking on the phone, 'Man, that's good, so what did he do? Ha ha ha... You bet! Great, you're a good one, that's for sure... he, he, that's great... you're a driver... you're a Schumacher, that's really something! Bang bang! You're a Fittipaldi!'

It went on until Kulaťak. Fucker spoke to me: 'Which street?'

'Which street?' I asked her.

'Kvar-tars... Kvar... Ma-vatarsk,' she answered. 'Ma-vatarsk.'

Fucker gave a pretentious sigh.

Mrs. Shapiro pinched my arm and spoke in a moist voice into my ear, 'Well, tell him to go straight and turn the corner over there and then right down to the end of the street.'

We reached the end of the street, got out and started walking along an unending, shadowy wall disappearing into the darkness. Just as I slammed the door of the car it started to pour.

We walked by wet villas. Stepped over dugout ditches bridged by swaying planks. Then we walked along an avenue that took us to a small shut-down factory of sorts. Half an hour later or so we got to deserted tennis courts. There the rain turned into a torrent. We stopped under a little roof of corrugated tin. Water gushed down from the eaves into an old tar barrel. The wind was bending poplars in the dark.

'I don't live here,' she said uncertainly. 'But it must be near... I hope.'

We started to walk back. We passed the shadowy wall again and walked through an unwelcoming villa neighbourhood lit by street lamps. We walked in silence. Suddenly I didn't feel like talking. What mattered most now was a cup of tea.

We were going through one of the numerous streets when she jumped, 'Oh, this is it! We're home!'

We went up the steps and unlocked the door. Behind

the door was a quiet, dry flat.

'I'm gonna take a shower,' she announced in the hall. 'And you come in and have a seat.'

I sat down in an armchair and looked at a large painting hanging on the wall. On it was a dancing Native American with red, blue, orange and violet spots. The dancer was a naked, ruffled, and grimacing woman with a gaping, luminescent dark-red pit between her dancing legs. On her stomach was a coiled up snake, or the like.

At that moment Mrs. Shapiro appeared in the doorway. She was carrying a tray with a steaming teapot and wearing a white robe which hardly covered her butt. An ancient sacrificial toga. I realised what she was attempting: to look like some idiotic Isadora Duncan. And she did. She noticed me looking at the painting.

'My best friend did that,' she said innocently. 'And the woman in the painting is me. That's how she sees me.'

'Hmm,' I answered, quite startled now.

After several cups of tea I went to the washroom to relieve myself. There I swayed from side to side for a bit while observing a fellow with blood-shot eyes in the mirror. 'You better keep your mouth shut!' I told him. When I returned there was a neat sofa made of piled-up mattresses right in the middle of the room. Incense was burning on the table.

'It's late. Let's go to bed,' she announced and dropped her toga. Under the toga her body was completely covered with tattoos. Her shoulders, her forearms, her back. There was a snake on her stomach. The tip of its tail was coiled up around her belly-button and it looked like it was basking in the sun on a rock. Its treacherous head was quietly resting under her left breast.

'That's a snake,' I stated.

'Oh, no, that's a symbol of snake power,' she differed and moved her stomach so that I would see the power in action. The snake became alive. I patted it. Her stomach was smooth, hot and hard as a rock.

'How is this possible,' I asked her. 'You're a mother of two.'

'Just like that,' she slapped her stomach with pleasure. 'That's America!'

'How do you mean "America"?' I wanted to know.

'America is simply America...'

I see, I get it. Nutrition, health care, life expectancy. Decoding the Book of Life. Science. Tradition. And human rights. Sure, foxy lady. And without further ado I took my pants off and pulled out a crumpled-up spider.

'Eek!' she feigned surprise.

Then we fell on the sofa and did what people do in such situations. Suddenly she conjured up a small basket overflowing with coloured condoms, 'Sorry, but we need to use this.'

'I see,' I responded. 'That's not gonna work..'

'Why not?'

'You know it squeaks and that makes me laugh and I can't concentrate. And I'd like to spare you that,' I lied. Really I was afraid that my libido would fail me and that I would not be able to turn off my brain, messed up by endless conversation.

'No, no, no, no, no,' she stated. 'It's gonna work!'

'I'm really sorry but I don't think so.'

'Yes, yes, yes, yes, yes,' she said resolutely and attempted to put it on me. I felt like a tipsy teenage girl picked up at a dance.

'No,' I said.

'No?'

'No.'

'OK then not,' she said and swiftly threw the whole basket out the open window. The colourful little packs flew out into the night, sparkled in the light from the street lamps like a swarm of exotic beetles, fell through the rain-drenched cherry-tree tops dark in the night and landed on the grass.

I wrestled with her unruly little body and at intervals studied her body decor. It was mostly too art nouveau-ish and overdone, but I was getting to like the snake more and more. Eventually I was no longer aware of where I was and with whom. Determined Mrs. Shapiro vanished some place and all that was left was an ordinary woman who was less afraid of dying than what precedes it: forgetting.

'Hey, tell me honestly,' I said when we'd finished.

'Yep?'

'How old are you?'

'There's no way I'm gonna tell you that!' she said in a hoarse voice, lay down on top of me, put her pinkies into my ears and fell asleep. I closed my eyes and listened to the wavering hum rising from the bottom of a lift shaft in the depths below my head. Before long I felt myself slowly descending there with the Californian on my stomach.

When I opened my eyes, she was already up and running around the house, naked. I watched her for a while. She looked like a doll scribbled upon in pencil. She was running back and forth, scratching herself with her tattooed hand right in her bushy bear's ear without any inhibition and humming to herself. Everything about her was small and firm and tight. I was getting to like her. She started to seem incredibly attractive. Except that she had those orderly, grey, practical eyes of hers again. It's always been like that. It typically seemed most interesting the moment it was over.

'I'm Rebecca,' she announced when she noticed I was awake. 'Do you want some coffee?'

I nodded and just as she was passing the couch, I pulled her back under the blanket. She held up her behind for me and waited until I was finished. Then she got up, kissed my cheek like some aunt and went to make coffee. After coffee I said goodbye.

It was still raining a bit outside. At the same time there was that autumn glare shining through the gardens. Lumps of mist wandered among the thuja trees and dried shoots with the odd puckered-up tomato hanging from them. Everything was sharp and clear and had a sense of urgency. There were fiery toadstool mushrooms of accurate and precise words springing up on everything. The dark, leathery egg of the primary word, about to burst, was hanging over the world. I was overcome with a strange and joyful feeling of calm. This led me to conclude that I still had too much alcohol in my body for the usual methods of sobering-up to work and the best thing to do would be to take a walk.

From around the corner emerged a hunched fellow in a thick rubber raincoat from which a folded fishing rod poked out. He was wearing a noticeably sweaty felt hat with badges on it. In his wake lingered a trace of the beautiful old-time smell of smoke, sweat, Vaseline, hand-cleanser, fish, and yesterday's beers and drinks. I started to follow the scent like a hound dog and without any plan went straight up to him, attracted by his ordinariness, his normality.

'Hello,' I said.

'Howdy…'

'Would you know how to get to Kulat'ák?'

I knew the answer but I couldn't help asking. I needed to talk.

'How to get there? Well, straight through these houses, then hang a left and you're there, eh?'

'Thanks. What about fish? Catching any in this weather?'

'Oh, man, it's been a shitty catch…' he said and proudly showed the content of a waxy bag he pulled out from under his raincoat. Inside were the scaly round yellowish bellies of fish rolling about. On top lay two gutted eels.

'This from the Vltava?' I marveled.

'Absolutely, mister!' I offered him a cigarette. The guy took a drag and continued, 'There are places in the Vltava with catfish that still remember President Masaryk! They're more intelligent than people; you can trust me on that. And carp? That big! These carp are the size of a St. Bernard, but you gotta know what you're doing! If you don't know what you're doing, you'll come back empty-handed! It's like with everything...'

'You're right,' I said. 'I used to work at the Libeň Island waterworks and sometimes early morning I'd stroll by the banks – you know the dead-end streams – and there you'd sometimes hear a splash at four in the morning like there was a calf rolling in the water. And when I looked there, I could only see something disappearing from the surface that may have been a carp if carp were the size of a dog-house...'

'Well, there you go.' The guy became uneasy. 'You a fisherman?'

My gaze drifted down to the bag propped against the curb. There was the jerk of a fin from its depths.

'Oh, no, I'm just saying what I saw.'

'In Libeň, huh,' he pondered. 'That might actually have been a catfish, mister! That wouldn't surprise me!'

'It's possible.'

The man blew out an uneven ribbon of smoke, bent down, picked up the bag and stuffed it back under his raincoat, 'That must've been a honkin' mother of a catfish, mister! No doubt. A whopping catfish! So to Kulat'ák, it's left, and then straight!'

'See ya,' I said, but the guy had already disappeared behind a lilac bush.

It started to rain more again. I went around the dark dormitory buildings that stood in the veils of rain like discarded battle ships on the Kola peninsula. The famed crest of the International Hotel floated in the low clouds nearby. I sat down on a bench. A toad sitting in a puddle half a metre from my shoe was studying me closely. I pulled out a cigarette and lit up.

A police car lurched out from behind some bushes, then slowed down as it spotted me. It drove by at walking pace, then pulled onto the pavement beside me. There were two of them, and you could tell they wanted to hassle someone, but at the same time they didn't feel like getting out into the rain. They were slowly chewing and staring impassively. They aped, with great precision, what they had seen in the stupidest films. Just sat there staring. Perhaps if I suddenly started to produce litres of jelly-like slime and turned into a disgusting Hollywood gargoyle in front of their very eyes, if I turned into a primordial combination of a zombie, a newt and an intelligent praying mantis and started to beat my flappy wings, it would not surprise them all that much. *That*, they were familiar with. But someone sitting on a bench in the rain, having a smoke, seemed unusual and suspect.

I was slowly getting cold but I was not going to make them happy by getting up and leaving. I lit up another one. The toad was still blinking at me from the puddle. Then it turned around awkwardly, moved its backside and crawled away. The police patiently waited until I finished smoking. When I finally put the cigarette out they started the car and drove away.

I was back at Kulat'ák, back to my old life. Sadness arrived, the king of all emotions. It was closely followed by my toothache again. I decided to get some more sleep and, as soon as I woke, to call the dentist. And tonight I'll stay home because they're showing *The Submarine Hunt* on TV.

# On Flying Objects

'I WAS SORTING things out at the cottage the other day and I found a pack of *ligeros* tucked behind some books and I thought of you,' said Vojta, passing a warped pack over his shoulder. 'They're a bit dry by now – they must have sat there for fifteen years, if not more – but they're still good old *liggies!*'

Feeling more than a little moved, I inspected the intimately familiar small golden sailboat on its dark bluish purple background.

'Dude, I really appreciate this,' I said. 'You mind if I light one up right now?'

'Go right ahead,' said Vojta. 'Monička hates it but I bet for you she'll make an exception...'

'That's crap, ever since you quit smoking you're the one who's been fucking nervous, it doesn't bother me,' responded Monička. 'I don't miss it!'

'Well, I don't need to, really,' I said.

'Go ahead and light up, Vojta will tough it out, right, he's got incredible willpower.'

'Shit, just light up, OK,' said Vojta. 'And why not give Monička one to keep her quiet.'

I stretched out my arm.

'No, thanks,' squeaked Monička.

'It's all right, I can wait,' I said.

'Come on, man, it's cool,' said Vojta.

'It's cool,' repeated Monička.

*Screw you then*, I thought to myself, flicked the lighter and inhaled the smoke. It tasted like I was smoking a ten-year-old magazine. But it was *ligeros*, a *liggie*, the cigarette of my youth. I was parked on the back seat of Vojta's old Escort, the front seat being reserved for Monička so that they could fight. They were always fighting. Quite often physically. When it came over them, they didn't care if there was a third person around; on the contrary, in a way they were glad. They actually rarely ever hurt each other since they each weighed only fifty-five kilos. They were like two struggling moths. Like two stuffed toys pushing each other around. It's true that I once witnessed Vojta throwing Monička through a glass door that separated a room and a hallway after he'd dragged her around the flat by her hair for a few minutes, before she retaliated by smashing a Chinese porcelain vase against his head, but that was more of an exception. They both then spent the rest of the day gluing the vase back together, working in unison like Poo and Eeyore because it had been a gift and I was helping them out.

We were on our way to a village near Kladno to visit their friends who were making goulash from a fallow deer that somebody's stepfather had shot in the Šumava mountains. The sun was setting above the Ruzyně part of Prague. The sky resembled a continuous slow-moving Plexiglas that someone had puked on. Vojta and Monička were barking at each other. I was looking past them, ahead. We were descending upon a valley full of sheet metal halls, bushes, piles of rotting wooden planks and empty cable reels.

'Stop swerving, you know I hate that,' said Monička.

'I'm not swerving, I'm zigzagging.'

'Then stop your zigzagging for God's sake!' Monička raised her voice.

'But you were praising me the other day in front of Pavlucha, saying how safe a driver I was.'

'I must've been pretty stupid!'

'You must've been,' added Vojta, turning the wheel back and forth.

'Stop swerving, you arsehole!'

'If you go on like this much longer, Monička, I swear to God I'm gonna drop you off right here,' said Vojta softly. 'And you can hitchhike back home for all I care.'

'Fine, stop the car, at least I won't be there when you two flip over somewhere! Stop the car!'

It's true that Vojta and I had drunk about a litre of vodka between us.

I was looking around the landscape. Suddenly I noticed a peculiar thing. On the overcast sky to the right of the windscreen five purple lines were glowing. Three were long, lined up side-by-side, and above those were two short ones. The strange thing about them was, they wouldn't stay in one place and kept quivering and flickering, so it was hard to focus on them to be able to say with certainty that they were there. If they were the navigation lights of a commercial plane or the reflectors of a helicopter, I thought, they would be moving in one direction and not jumping around like that. Strange. Strange.

'Stop the car, did you hear me, I'm out of here!' reached my ears.

'Look Monička, stop making trouble and sit down or else I'm really gonna drop you off, I swear to God!'

'Well, get to it!'

'It wouldn't bother me, you're always on my case anyway!'

'You're on mine, OK?'

The lines loomed up below the smoky ceiling of the landscape, shimmering lightly. I was inhaling smoke and trying not to lose sight of them, which wasn't that simple since they periodically jumped behind a tree or a warehouse. I took another *ligeros*.

'I have to listen to this prattle all the time,' said Vojta. 'From dusk to dawn you burden my brain.'

'I burden your brain?'

'Yeah, you burden my brain with totally useless

information!'

'I'm surprised you can actually take it in through all that booze!'

'The thing is that it's *all* I can do! But I can't think! My brain is mucked up with bullshit!'

'Hm... I really wonder why you need to think,' Monička ruminated.

'You would be surprised, but there's quite a lot to think about in the world!' stated Vojta.

The lines were at that moment hovering between two silver chimneys. Suddenly they began to move and flew over to the right, so I could now see them through the side window. I rolled down the window and stared at them. The colour of the lights could best be described as purple with an occasional hint of red. At least that's how it appeared to me. To be honest, I didn't experience any extraordinary feelings. It all somehow fitted together. The mess around us, the sunset, the fight in front, the ancient *ligeros*, and those flickering lines above.

The lights were slowly moving above the landscape, dancing among the clouds, keeping their original formation: three down, two up. One moment they disappeared behind a cloud and the next moment they showed up further away. It was as if their colour paled and broke into a shade of pink from time to time, but then returned back to the original purple. By now I had to turn to see them through the back window. Then they vanished behind the crown of a walnut tree.

I was seized by the memory of a day long ago, when I was sitting just like this in the back seat of an old black Tatra driven by a certain Mr. Kabrna in a leather jacket with the collar turned up, an aging dandy with a protruding lower lip and slicked back grey hair, a former RAF pilot, with my grandpa Zdenek sitting beside him. They had met in jail while pouring concrete for a railway underpass. We were going back through the night, gramps and Kabrna debating something and me sitting and looking around. I must have been about four. Empty landscape slowly passed by, yellowy-lit clusters of settlements changed their configurations in the distance, a mysterious city light loomed just above the horizon and stars were being cooked in the oily sky. The Tatra was bobbing up and down in a black pit surrounded by phosphorescent ant-hills. I saw that I landed in a world which was not only incomprehensible, but which defied any description, since its very essence kept changing every minute. I was in a wondrous cave.

'Make it no less than six cubic metres, Mr. Motejl,' said my gramps, when it was still daylight, to a white-haired rustic in overalls in the courtyard of some warehouse, where bags and bricks and sacks were being piled up, and those cubic metres must have been the reason for our trip, since this was the time when my gramps was building a house. 'Make it no less than six cubic metres, Mr. Motejl...' And driving around our lot was Emil ämíd, a forever smiling, and perhaps slightly retarded, working man; Emil Šmíd on a Lanz tractor, a rusty blue stegosaurus with a bulbous funnel belching out sweet gas fumes, driving bricks and pulling beams around our lot; scary Emil ämíd, with black teeth with holes in them, famed for never having anything for lunch but Emmental with butter, a thick slice of Emmental with a thick layer of butter and no bread.

Nothing much has changed in my life since then. The same electric lights are still floating in the distance. The same lives are lived there. It's no more understandable than back then. Only perhaps slightly less surprising.

'Fuck it, I can just turn the car around right now!' said Vojta, in a voice that was by now quite loud.

'Well, you can't 'cuz what would the guys think if this Vojta dude didn't turn up, what would they do there without you…,' a venomous, low little voice was scratching at my eardrum. I actually liked Monička, but only when Vojta was not around. And I liked Vojta even better, but without Monička.

Alas! What happened to those lines, I thought to myself. I turned my head from side to side, but I couldn't find them. They were gone. The moon was floating among the clouds.

That reminded me of the one-eyed cat called Lojza I used to have at the Lhotka waterworks. When he was a kitten, his own mother scratched out one of his eyes, and I would then put some *framykoin* ointment on its hollow socket and, thanks to that, without really wanting to, I managed to bring myself up a hairy little son, who was constantly milling about my feet or sitting behind my neck and staring into a book with me, or slowly suffocating me, anxiously wrapped around my head when I was trying to fall asleep at three in the morning. So this Lojza would, at full moon, manage to sit all night and watch the moon. Any other time he would spring up and get to me in no time, so that he would stay with me for the rest of my shift, not leaving me for a minute, not even when I was on the bog and he would paw at the door and meow until I opened it. But at full moon he would turn his back on me, take a seat on the window sill and with his one eye watch the pale plate sliding among the stars for hours and hours, sighing, raising his eyebrows and sadly, mysteriously, shuddering. How is it – Jakub Deml might have asked half a century ago – that we can be so arrogant as to think that we are differentiated from other beings by having a soul. But all I could do – sitting in the back of Vojta's old Escort that night, from the 14th to the 15th of September, 2000 – was to take another mummified *ligeros*. And that's just what I did.

'*I got into a park, / Sat down on a bench, / Closed my eyes and saw / A yellow dog about to bark…*' crowed Vojta out of the blue and hit the wheel and honked boisterously.

'*Wide-eyed he stared at me, his bared teeth I can see, / Thinks maybe I am his bone, I've had enough of this drone! / Get lost you bitch, get lost you bitch, / Get lost you bitch, get lost you bitch!*' I joined in.

Vojta kept honking, turning the wheel, zigzagging with us from hard shoulder to hard shoulder.

'*Get lost you bitch!* (beep, beep!)*, get lost you bitch!* (beep, beep!)*, get lost you bitch* (beep, beep!)*, get lost you bitch!* (beep, beep!)...'

The Escort was rocking along the roadway like a barge on the sea.

'Concentrate on the road, please,' begged Monicka.

'That's exactly what we're doing, this is a part of concentrating,' said Vojta.

'So don't kill us while you're at it!'

'I need a way to relax so I won't kill you.'

'You're a real retard!'

'Yeah, that must be about right, otherwise I wouldn't have...'

'What wouldn't you have? Well, what wouldn't you have?!'

'Can't you shut up for just one minute, Monička! Do you have to keep on yakking!'

'Me! That's good!'

'Yeah, you! You sow seeds of discord in the soul! You're impossible! It's in your genes!'

'Well, fuck you...!' said Monicka in astonishment.

'See, that's it, that's what I mean, you can't keep your mouth shut for a moment!'

'*I'm* impossible! Well fuck you ten times over!'

'You *are* impossible. And on top of that you're...'

'What am I? What am I on top of that?! What am I, you little shit?!'

'You're incredibly *boring*, if you wanna hear it!'

'What!'

'Yeah, you heard right! Same thing every day! All the

time! "You never do this... you never do that...!"'

'So why are you with me? Why the fuck are you with me?'

'Don't know!' said Vojta and shifted to third gear.

We drove in silence for about ten minutes. The body of the car swallowed lit-up dust from the road. On the left appeared a bushy, low black forest. All of a sudden, a roe deer leapt out of the forest onto the road. The animal's eyes shone like light bulbs in the headlights. It froze in fright. The car missed it by a few inches.

'Aach!' Monička screamed out.

'Dude,' grumbled Vojta. 'That was close...'

Then there was silence. Little drops of rain started to land on the windscreen. The headlights were licking a line of poplars.

'Well, everybody gets by in their own way,' said Vojta abruptly.

Then there was silence again. Only the squeaking of the wipers could be heard.

'I saw a UFO a while ago,' I said, to break the silence.

'That's what I see every day,' responded Monicka. 'I'm actually married to one!'

'Where are we, anyway?' pondered Vojta.

Monička peered at a map, 'I think we need to hang a right now, then there should be a level-crossing gate and a connection to a main road, and then straight.'

We turned right. Soon, fenced off yards, concrete panels, and houses with fallen off facades turned up everywhere. A few jolly blokes in overalls almost jumped right in front of our car, at a curve. I spotted kicked-in teeth, tattooed necks, gin-soaked mouths, drunk eyes. At the next curve gypsy children sat on a railing, fiercely chewing and shouting something. Further on a horribly fat woman in an apron was pushing herself through the darkness while threatening someone out of sight.

'We're clearly in Kladno,' remarked Vojta.

'We're clearly in deep shit,' responded Monička.

'But whose fault is that, I ask?'

'Mine, of course!'

'Well, that's highly likely... If you had looked at the map earlier on, we wouldn't be in deep shit now,' recited Vojta with a peculiar half-smile, as if trying to suppress some secret, uneasy pleasure. 'You'd better give it to Honza!'

Monička thrust the map into my hands. Vojta passed me a torch. Ah, relationships. I was glad that this time it wasn't my own. I straightened out the map and darted about the paper with my light.

In the meantime we had driven into an odd, wide street lined on both sides by large, windowless buildings. There were street lights, a road, even if it was a bumpy one, and all around, huge brick windowless houses. It was like going down a street with nothing but mausoleums on either side. Then the buildings ended and all we could do was drive through a wrecked iron gate into a deserted area where the road ended. Further on was just black gravel and some tracks. Out of the darkness rose the outlines of metal structures that carried dark pipes into the distance. It was as if we found ourselves in the stomach of an extremely large fossilized being. Rusty guts twirled high above us. Further on gigantic concrete vertebrae were strewn about. Smoke was rolling above greasy puddles.

'Wow man, this looks like a different planet,' breathed Vojta and turned off the engine.

That same moment a shot rang out somewhere close. And another one. I could clearly hear the whizz of the bullet. A moment later a guy emerged from the darkness holding gun in both hands.

'Freeze!' he roared and pointed at Vojta's head. 'Free' he bellowed again.

'I am,' said Vojta quietly.

'What are you doing here? Quick!'

We searched for a suitable answer.

'What are you doing here? Pronto!' repeated the guy.

'Well, what are we doing here...?' said Vojta.

The man walked around the car while aiming at us.

'Please,' piped up Monička in a shaky voice.

'No please! I'm asking what you're doing here!'

'Please... can I light up?'

The man stooped and looked at Monička.

'You're a woman?' he said.

'Yeah, and please can I light up?'

'Light up what?!'

'What do you mean, light up what?'

'What do you want to light up?' barked the man and, perhaps without realizing it, pointed the shooter at her. He simply pointed at whomever he happened to be speaking to.

'Like what do you mean, what do I want to light up...' Monicka started to sob. 'A cigarette, damn it!'

'Okay, smoke!' ordered the man.

The lighter only worked on the fifth try. I watched her trembling hand with fascination.

'So what are you doing here! Fast!' he turned to Vojta again.

'We're looking for the road to Ledce,' I added to the debate.

'Yeah, right!' he aimed at me, white spit spraying from his mouth. 'So you're looking for a road here, right!' I inspected the shiny muzzle and felt a small cold hand grab my stomach. It felt like I had a raw pig's leg in my belly. That, strangely, comforted me somehow.

'Yeah, here,' I said.

'A likely story!'

'Look,' Vojta pulled himself together. 'Are you some sort of watchman here or something?'

'Security guard,' barked the man and aimed at him again.

'Well, this must be a mistake—'

'No mistake!' The moron got angry and, as he spluttered all over himself, it became obvious that psychological balance was not one of his virtues. 'There's an operation in progress here! What are you doing here? Make it quick!'

'We're looking for the road,' I said again.

For a moment it felt like he didn't know what to do next.

'Driver out!' He finally worked it out and took a few steps back. 'Open the trunk!'

Vojta got out and opened the trunk. The guard shone his torch in for a long time. At the same time he held his shooter up in our general direction.

'Holy f-f-fuck…' Monička started to cry.

'Stop bawling,' I said quietly. 'Or he'll really lose it!'

I was far from calm myself. But, finding myself in such an unbelievable situation, where everything seemed so distant from anything one normally expects, I was able to follow events with a certain detached curiosity.

Vojta shut the trunk and the jerk ordered him to 'Get back!'

'So what to do with you!' he continued. 'You have no business being here!'

'Why don't we go then,' suggested Vojta.

'How do you mean go?! Where?'

'Away,' whispered Monička.

'Make it snappy then!' barked the security guard.

Vojta started the engine, put it in reverse and started backing up. The man followed us, still aiming at the windscreen. Only now did we have a chance to take a good look at him. He was a small town type, with sticky-out ears and a simple mug – a bandy-legged dip-shit with a shaved head. He was wearing what looked like black overalls, with several bulging pockets. Perhaps he had grenades there. Who knows. He followed us all the way to the wrecked gate, stopped there and stared at us. We continued to reverse for about twenty more metres. Then Vojta slowly turned around and we were back on that strange street with no windows.

'Screw you, stupid fuckhead!' Vojta became bold when we were far enough away. 'Monička, would you give me a cigarette?'

'I only had one, Vojta, my dear. If you had said anything I would have been happy to give it to you...'

'Have a *liggy*,' I offered.

'No way, those are for you.'

'Grab one, don't be silly.'

'All right, thanks,' said Vojta and Monička lit his cigarette with a shaking hand.

'Would you mind if I had one, too?' She turned back. I gave her a cigarette and looked inside the pack. Only one left. I pulled it out and lit up. The three of us all blew out smoke.

'Now I'm completely sober for sure,' Vojta ventured in an unsteady voice.

'Me, too, no doubt about it,' I said.

Monička was silent for a while, the end of her *ligeros* red-hot.

We drove in silence again. Dry, pleasant-smelling smoke was filling up the car. After a while I turned the torch on again and started to study the map. I saw trembling dark red snaking roads, green cross-hatching and blue veins and numerous signs and letters and lines and spots. Names of villages began to willfully break apart and merge in front of my eyes: Jedozda, Čelesuty, Hulora Srzdeň...

'Vojta, would you be a darling and stop for me for a moment?' squeaked Monička.

'Absolutely, my Monička, shall I do that right away?'

'Yeah,' Monička sobbed, grabbing her stomach, and as soon as she was two steps away from the car, the retching sound began.

'Can I help you in any way?' worried Vojta.

'S'allrigh... blua... thanks, Vojta... blua, bluea... blua...' Her beautiful white hand, with its black painted nails sticking out of the rolled-up sleeve of a black shirt, waved in the dark. Black and red checkered pants fitted tightly around her goat pelvis. This type of subdued elegance has always been Monička's thing. She was leaning against a sign that limited the speed to eighty kilometres per hour while a gurgling came from inside her. The bare trunks of a sparse forest stuck out of the horizon, as monotonously blinking fluorescent lights running alongside some kind of warehouse or factory shone through them.

'Now we're really fucked,' noted Vojta.

'No we're not, I got it,' I said. 'Here, Ledce! Straight to Smečno and left at the first intersection, it's close, not even five kilometres...'

Finally we reached a low, large farmhouse with all of its lights on. Small groups of people walked about the garden. There was a bonfire. Music playing. Dancing couples were rocking in the shimmering light. Someone threw a log onto the fire. A sheaf of sparks exploded between the trees. Fiery threads shot to the sky.

A dazzled redheaded guy in shorts stepped into the beam of light and gave us a big smile. When we stopped, he shouted, 'Hi! Vojta! Vojta's here! You've really come at a good time! Everything's been gobbled up! There's only some salami and plum brandy left... Would you like some?'

'Yeah!' we all said in unison.

# Sultry

I WAS THIRTY minutes late, so I turned onto Kaprova Street and cut across the old town square even though it was mid-July and crowds of heat-dazed tourists were blundering all around. I zigzagged among them, trying not to bump into anyone if at all possible, eventually realizing there was no way around it. 'Pardon me...' I kept repeating to the clusters of loudly chattering figures, 'pardon me, pardon me!'

I felt my sweat-soaked t-shirt sticking to my back. Drop after drop was rolling down my spine. After a while I gave up and with the full strength of my body began to forge my way through the tightly closed ranks of yakking broad-shouldered blond men spreading themselves out across the whole pavement, since − as I knew already − these types wouldn't move out of my way no matter what. I then began to pull them apart with my hands. I was surprised to notice that they allowed themselves to be pushed aside without much resistance. 'Martians!' I kept repeating to the laughing, flat, relaxed faces, and my heart was rattling. 'Martians!'

I brushed up against the corner of an open shop to cut ahead of a bunch of merry fashionistas. In that instant I was struck, as if clubbed over the head, by the sound of some sweetly familiar music coming out of the hollows of the shop. I stopped and listened. It was the freemasonic clucking from *The Magic Flute*: 'Pa... pa, pa... pa, pa Pa-pa-pa-pa-pa-papagena! Pa-pa-pa-pa-pa-papageno!' It frightened me how well I understood what was going on: I was listening to a commentary on the endless moving and shifting and wandering and heaving. A prayer sung by a living mass that fears to look ahead, so instead it makes faces sideways in the mirror. 'O Isis und Osiris!' And what's worse: even in a moment when blood is already oozing somewhere in the slacks, and one's cells, tired of the same old routine, begin to act whatever way they please, the shoes get even more polished, and the stiff ill-fitting wig is being fluffed up. I stood and listened. The strings' pizzicato was blending in with the flapping of wings above the red-hot roofs. After all, this was composed only a few months before its creator was himself thrown into a pit. 'Papagena! Papageno!'

I glimpsed my own reflection in the shop window. The thought ran through my brain: you're feeling like a ghost here yourself. Like someone who essentially no longer exists but continues to deceive others with his physical presence, covering his tracks, and inventing naïve lies to keep others in the dark... In that moment a tiny man in baggy pants slammed into me with his shoulder. 'Parrrdonn!' he shouted. I groaned and continued on with the flow again. I passed the group of shouting fashionistas once more.

The mouse hole of a street beside the Týn Cathedral was completely jammed up. Dozens of tour groups were gathering there, fiddling with their video cameras. There were hats, puppets, trinkets, mugs, junk, and Russian dolls for sale at different booths. I made my way along the wall, stepping over outlandishly dreadlocked youths sitting on the ground with their legs stretched out onto the tiny street to show just how mellow they were. Chatter and laughter resounded all around.

An older moustachioed fellow was standing motionless in the middle of Týnská Street, holding open a folder with a menu from some newly opened restaurant. He was holding it so that the freckled, lumpy gals in shorts, chaperoned by pale two-metre-tall old men, along with the stoned Spanish youths, the Japanese grandmothers in bonnets, and the screaming Anglo-Saxon redheaded lasses could see what bargains were available. The fellow stood there looking ahead and the crowd rolled over him.

And seeing all this around me – this consequence of the tourist industry, this cheerful, innocent, deodorant-wearing crowd with its childlike curiosity, that didn't give a damn that the world was about to fall apart right under its nose because it wouldn't happen today, and it wouldn't happen tomorrow, and perhaps not even the day after that – all of a sudden everything went black before my eyes.

I approached the man and said, 'Aren't you ashamed of yourself?'

The man turned his grey eyes to me. His face was full of tiny wrinkles. His receding hair was greying and slicked back. His irises reflected the towering Týn Cathedral, which looked like a spacecraft ready to launch, the commercial towing spaceship *Nostromo* dashing through foreign, empty, dizzyingly remote space. The spires protruded, like two dried-up marker pens, into a sky full of motionless clouds.

'Of course I am,' he answered.

'I see,' I said, 'I'm sorry in that case.'

'You don't need to be,' replied the man and continued holding the open menu.

My eyes glanced over the prices: 499 korun... 548 korun... 829 korun...

'Bye then,' I said and headed away.

'Izit gud vej tu visit dis big cherch?'An incredibly cute bespectacled Asian girl approached me with a smile, and five other equally cute, bespectacled, smiling girls aligned behind her.

'Yes, it is.' I waved my arm and attempted a smile myself.

The girls bowed slightly, and I bowed slightly as well. For a second my eyes followed six firm, agile bums and six pairs of white adidas shoes walking away from me, down the street towards the cathedral, which from here looked even more like a worn-out spaceship battered by meteorites, hung with dozens of antennae pointed in the direction of the flight into an icy universe.

I turned and hurried on. There was a piece of poo in the shape of Sleeping Beauty resting by the curb in front of Café Týn. Although my running late was getting out of hand, I had to stop once more; I stood there looking at the thing. It was unbelievable. The likeness to the human body was frighteningly perfect. There was a tiny, wistful houri with a dim luster, and a hip nonchalantly protruding, lying on the cobblestones a metre away from the sole of my shoe. A naked odalisque, with a large, smooth, beautifully parted behind, and a small tilted head.

When I grabbed the door-handle at the café twenty seconds later, it turned out that Tomáš was waiting for me unruffled, one leg crossed over the other, sipping a beer, reading a thick book wrapped in a newspaper.

# An Oddball

ANDULA HAD THE strangest figure; she had the chest of a little mackerel, although her legs and behind were those of a real woman. So when I saw her standing outside a shop-window on the other side of the street, I knew without a doubt it was her. Without thinking twice I sped up. Going out for a glass of wine with Andula, whom I hadn't seen in at least eight years, was a perfect opportunity not to have to worry about anything else for the moment.

'Howdy,' she intoned as if we saw each other almost every day.

We took a seat in the restaurant 'At Anežka's' and tested each other for a while by recalling old stories.

'And what else?' I inquired after we got through all of them.

'Nothin',' she sighed. 'There's always somethin' but it always amounts to one big zilch, the last one a guy called Jozifek.'

'And?'

'And nothing, as usual. Maybe by now I should just forget it and get me to a nunnery and busy myself watering pansies.'

'Right, that sounds like you. So what about this Jozifek guy?'

'What about him? A good man, not thick, everything hunky dory, he was a bit introverted, quiet and shy, but I liked that, you know. The only weird thing was that although he claimed to have his own place, we'd only ever go to mine and he never invited me over. So eventually

I asked him without being too conspicuous about it, you know me...'

I nodded. I knew just how *inconspicuous* she could be. Andula was forever left on the shelf; she was about thirty five, had a child and still wasn't able to find Mr. Right. She wasn't all that unattractive or stupid, and all things considered she was fun to be around. But as soon as it came to relationships or getting married, she'd lose her spark and sink into despair. She'd even have nightmares of a huge four-metre-tall dark man following her on the street puffing like a steam roller, thundering into the back of her neck: *You're impossible...! You're impossible...! Impossible...! You're impossible...!*

'So how did he respond?' I asked.

'He grew serious and said: You'd be interested in coming over to my place? And I said why not, and so he said he'd like to invite me over, and he uttered it so ceremoniously that it scared me a bit. All right, so I got all dressed up and headed over. I rang the bell, and he answered the door, talking like we were in a film: Come in! But he looked somehow ill at ease... So he brings me in, I sit down, look around, an ordinary flat, nothing abnormal, no ears in alcohol, no skulls with scribbles all over them, no dirty pictures. But somehow he was still strangely nervous... So, cheers!'

We clinked glasses and in the heat of the conversation Andula took off her jacket revealing her child-like shoulders to the world: 'And then I saw it! There were humongous book-cases with glass doors lining three of his walls, so I took a peek to see what he liked to read. And there was not a single book there. Those shelves were packed top to bottom with all sorts of models: tanks, armoured vehicles and caterpillar trucks. Would you believe it? Hundreds and thousands!'

'Really?'

'But if it were only tanks! Instead, he had all sorts of scenes set up there! Always a little board with a few tiny houses, one of them made to look like it had been charred, tiny beams and bricks scattered around, a complete street there with a tobacco shop, street lights, everything; and then there was a dead SS-man lying by the tobacco shop and American tanks around the corner, and there was a wall with Germans waiting behind it with a little canon to ambush the tanks. And there were tiny torn posters with swastikas on the wall, imagine... Or he had a scene set up there with tiny soldiers repairing a tank, one fiddling with the engine, another wiping his grimy hands on a rag, a third stripped topless with a hairy chest polishing his machine-gun and another one sitting on top of the turret eating bread with salami! A little loaf, *this* tiny – see!'

Then she described a soldier in a helmet sitting on a tank, wearing black-rimmed glasses, from behind which tiny light blue eyes looked at Andula, while another solder sat on an overturned jeep drinking coke from a can.

'Note that he's already drinking his second one,' commented Jozifek, his voice nervously cracking, 'Here's a crumpled one...' And indeed, a tiny squashed can was lying on the ground.

Another private was urinating beside a fence. That one had really attracted Andula's attention. She took a closer look. There was a tiny pale willy sticking out of his camouflaged pants with a translucent yellow stream arching into a shot-through helmet lying on the ground. 'He's pissing,' slipped through her lips. 'Yeah. That's a thread stretched out of transparent polystyrene over a flame,' Jozifek breathed, 'and I painted the thread transparent yellow so it would be realistic...'

'Tell me what else he had there,' I asked, feeling enchanted.

'We'd be here all night.' She waved her hand. 'He showed me each scene individually – one after the other for maybe three hours – and kept making tea, before finally opening a dusty bottle of whiskey, which must have been sitting on top of his wardrobe since the Christmas before last, and he kept telling me: Look here, see this is a German p-r-c-k-v three or whatever he called it, but what's really interesting is – notice it's got a completely different turret with a Russian canon on it. Why? Because it had been captured by the Russians and they modified it, and then the Germans recaptured it back again and put it back in their arsenal! And he pointed out this hideous beat-up monster to me that looked like a cow had pissed on it and a dog had licked it!'

'And how come you remember this in such detail?' I asked.

'What do you mean?'

'Those terms and such...'

'I used to act in theatre, so I'm used to memorizing things, didn't you know?'

'I see, and what else was there?'

'Shitloads of things, he was in his element, he was talking on and on and would fill up his whiskey to give him the strength to change the subject. And after three shots he got so hammered that he spent ten minutes trying to turn his TV on with his mobile... But why don't you tell me what you've been up to?'

'Same old, same old, not much to report... And after that you never saw him again?'

'What do you mean never saw him again, we were together for almost nine months! I was over at his place more than my own once he was sure I wouldn't look down on him because of his models... He had this corner and as soon as he got home, he'd sit down and start sawing and painting. Good stuff, I thought to myself. Don't be stupid. If he was in the habit of not showing up all night, and then calling in the morning – telling me in a conspicuously sweet voice that he'd slept over at work – that would be worse. This way at least you know where you can find him... So I pampered the guy, cooked for him, dusted. And while I was dusting one of those shelves, he suddenly jumped up: 'Jesus, not there!' It was a shelf where dusting was not allowed; he'd collect the dust there with a little brush and glue it onto his models to make them look worn-out from battle.'

'Imagine that.'

'Well... and then one day he took the three of us on a trip. I thought, that's good, things are looking up, he may even be a family man! So he loaded us into the car and took us to some place near Nový Bor. And when we arrived, guess what was there?'

I shrugged my shoulders even though I had an inkling.

'A gathering of military vehicles enthusiasts! A whole bunch of jeeps and trucks surrounded by morons dressed up as soldier-boys, and Jozifek would say hi to half of them and loiter and start chatting and I just stood there like a sawhorse! And the soldiers would run around the hills, you know, Germans against the Yankees. It was fucking hot, so they'd slack off on top of everything, and you'd always have some fat guy hiding behind the bushes gulping pop from his canteen. It was just demented... But Jozifek was head over heels into it; he'd watch with his binoculars and advise them: Let him come closer, don't shoot yet... reload and wait! And the highlight of the day was when a tank rolled out of a forest, stopped and fired. Jozifek was laughing ecstatically at that moment. And that was basically the last straw,' she sighed. 'Then a few days later we had a fight, and I was stupid enough to make him choose: me or his tanks! So I'm alone again...'

'Hmm,' I nodded. 'Care for another glass?'

'Why not get a carafe then?' opined Andula.


Before I knew it I was taking my shoes off in the hall of her flat. All of a sudden we were making mulled wine in the kitchen of a prefab high-rise. The gas was hissing and the little blue-green teeth of the flame nibbled on the bottom of the pot. The flu-season aroma of lemon, cloves and cinnamon permeated the air. When the mulled wine was ready, we each took a sip, left it on the table and went to bed. As soon as we touched each other, the switch flipped on just like years ago, getting almost too quickly to the top of the hill and then quickly downhill; only with Andula could it be so matter of fact.

'Now...' her voice sounded into the thickening fog of slumber.

'What?'

'Do I still have an amazing tummy, as you always used to say?'

'You do,' I said honestly. But she also had a web of varicose veins spreading on the back of her thighs and calves – I noticed when she was coming out of the bathroom. She used to have white and firm and smooth alabaster legs.

A sharp burning woke me in the middle of the night. For a while I lay there thinking what it could be. Then I couldn't stand it anymore and started scratching myself. The nerve endings soon became uncontrollably fired up. For some time I kept on brutally scratching and rubbing myself. Then the itching turned into pain.

Andula wriggled beside me: 'I have a bit of an infection, you know, yeast or something. Are you mad at me?'

'No.'

'It's nothing dangerous, you know, I'm taking care of it, don't worry, I use this awful cream...'

'That's all right, get some sleep.'

She began to snooze. After a while I felt her naughty hand tentatively grasping my dick. I tried to ignore it, thinking it looked like I was in enough trouble already. But when her other hand grabbed my balls from behind, my sore fellow obediently rose to attention again.

She woke me up at quarter to six: 'Look, I'm sorry but you gotta be getting up, Martínek is not so little anymore, you know... just so he won't find you in here...'

I did my amateur acting impression of sleeping hard.

'Do you hear me, get up!' she insisted and shook me. 'Martínek is sleeping next door, he already knows about this kind of stuff, you gotta go! Do you hear me!'

I got up, got dressed, had a sip of horribly cold mulled wine in the kitchen and closed the door behind me. On the way down the scratched green linoleum stairs, the memory occurred to me of how I used to visit this Andula in Vršovice, where she was renting a place in this low brick house; we would sit in the back yard, smoke, drink wine and watch the stars before giving way to bodily spontaneity. Once I left there in the middle of the night, after a squabble – I don't even remember what it was about – but we were right in the middle of fucking and I basically dashed out into the night like a headstrong idiot, and Andula ran out after me, stark naked, without a care. And she ran after me down the cobblestoned Voronêûská Street, among the parked Zhigulis, pitter-pattered behind me all the way down to the intersection, and as she was barefoot I didn't hear her and kept marching on with my shirt open. She caught up with me only a few metres before the Pilotů cinema, threw herself around my neck from behind and whispered into my ear in her moist bovine little voice: 'C'mon, don't be silly... don't be going anywhere, come back!' But that's at least twelve years ago now, maybe fifteen.

The morning breeze was blowing among the buildings. The jagged battlements of the city were slowly emerging out of a purple strip on the horizon. The sky looked like a snowy slope on the edge of town, criss-crossed with the tracks of children's sleds. My balls were so itchy I could hardly walk. I couldn't really scratch myself either, as I was surrounded by the usual demographics rushing to work.

A booth was open at the bus-stop. I bought a coffee in a polystyrene cup, sat down on a bench, and every time it was at all possible I quickly scratched.

A self-assured female redhead in a skirt with a slit walking a shaking, sleepy little pooch was passing by. The doggie scampered over, smelled my shoe, lifted its leg and sprayed a few drops onto my briefcase, which was leaning against the concrete foot of the bench.

The woman gave me a once over: 'Jesus, he's so stupid. Is that all right?'

So long as it's only a dog that does it, I thought to myself. That'll do.

'So long as it's only a dog that does it,' I answered.

'Let's go you fucking pig!' she ordered the dog.

Don't be looking there, I scolded myself in my mind. Don't be looking there, it's just so crude. Somehow it was in the family, though, whenever my father talked to a woman, he'd always take a look at her legs afterwards, same thing with gramps, same thing with my uncle. At least you should be mannerly! This turning one's head around! Drink your coffee, don't be scratching yourself and most of all don't be looking there!'

I turned my head in the direction the woman was heading. And what I saw was an almost two-metre tall, frightfully serious chicken walking towards me on its huge shaky claws, staring right at me. I got the heebie-jeebies. I soon realized though that this was just some poor fellow stuck in a costume to make some extra cash by promoting KFC.

# Daily Grind

*Many Eskimos and polar explorers also perished by driving their dog train straight over the summit of an iceberg, without suspecting that the hump gave way to a deep crevasse on the other side.*

Jan Welzl

I SET ASIDE Monday to write a short story, which for two weeks I'd been claiming to have already finished. I got up, cooked four eggs, popped them into a mug and splashed some ketchup on them. When I was gulping down the first bite, the telephone rang. They were calling from the editorial office to say they urgently needed the story.

'I still need to go through it with a fine-toothed comb, when do you need it by?' I said with as assertive a voice as possible.

'Tomorrow morning at the latest, that's the deadline.'

'No problem, I should be able to handle that.'

'What do you mean *should*, you've got to have it done! That's just your regular daily grind – you're a writer, right!'

Every time someone calls me that, I feel they're just taking the piss out of me. It had been my fourth year of sitting at home, blowing smoke into the lamp and writing instead of living.

'Yeah, I think so,' I answered.

'All right, so zip through it and let's see at least six standard pages of text by tomorrow morning!'

The job was for a supplement that actually paid well and without much hassle. So I drew the curtains, turned off the phone, settled down and started thinking what the short story should be about. The world suddenly seemed as desolate and dumb as a miniature, enamel-coated Karlštejn Castle[2] in someone's front yard.

The doorbell rang in less than an hour. I stared ahead motionlessly for a bit; I had only once before been able to not answer the door, in the spring of 1996, when someone rang the doorbell at ten in the evening and kept on ringing for the longest time, maybe fifteen minutes, while I was lying on the couch reading *The History of the Conquest of Mexico*. I never did find out who it was back then.

The doorbell screeched again. I went and answered it.

'Hi!' a friend said. 'Your phone is turned off, right?'

'Yeah, so?'

'Well nothing, if you don't mind that I've been waiting for you at Jiřího z Poděbrad Square for forty five minutes! We were gonna grab a beer!'

'I'm sorry, I forgot,' I smacked my forehead with my palm. 'The last few weeks my cylinders haven't been firing too well.'

'That's all right, I've also been living basically... Whatcha got there?' my friend inquired, peeking into my mug from afar like into the barrel of a mortar.

'Eggs. You soft-boil them, crack 'em open, get them out with a spoon, add salt, pepper, soy sauce, shredded cheese, ham, onions, anything in that vein, give it a stir and it's ready. That's all we ever had for breakfast during my last marriage.'

'Just that it's all red.' He was not convinced.

'It's ketchup.'

'That was with Bláňa, right? The big-eyed one?'

'Well, yeah.'

'Listen, do you mind if I have a little taste... just a spoonful?'

We finished off the eggs. My friend pulled out a dusty magazine from a shelf and leafed through it. 'Ha-ha, listen

2. Famous national landmark in Central Bohemia.

to this,' he said. '"The feelings in an underwater craft are hereby described by an English sailor: while submersed, one feels strangely moved and excited, thereafter falling into a sort of daze. Later, anxiety and lethargy occur, perhaps as a consequence of knowing one is completely helpless. Seasickness essentially does not loosen its grip on you under water. By spending an extended period of time in an underwater craft, the crew lose their colour and pale, the cause of which may be the bad air which fills the entire space of the craft shortly after the descent into the depths of the ocean..."' he quoted. 'Nineteen o seven...!'

Laughter came out of me, and as usual I felt somehow deficient – I've always had the feeling that just because someone is directly conversing with me I have to reward them with more entertainment than I am capable of at that moment; that I'm unable to deliver what's expected of me. That sooner or later, therefore, everyone will conclude that I'm an idiot.

We put on our shoes and went out. Smelly refuse poured out of a knocked-over rubbish bin. A piece of torn-up pantyhose was flapping in a Robinia tree. The TV transmitter tower was being ascended by three-metre laminate babies, the result of a sculptor's decorative outbursts.

'These fucking babies really bug the hell out of me.' I pointed to the tower.

'These are just some karmic illusions, I just ignore it!' My friend waved his hand. 'Bothering humanity with their ambitions... a bunch of arseholes... a kick in the head is what those cunts need... a waste of time thinking about it... artists!'

We went down Ruská Street without haste, traversed the hill by the Vršovice Townhall, and headed down the meandering little streets towards Nusle. An ambulance was speeding down the street. The siren was wailing psychotically. As far as you could hear, there were sounds – honking, chirping, squeaking, banging, barking, rattling, howling, busyness. Residences leaned over damp vacant spaces where piles of old pots and mouldy coats were quietly relinquishing life under the shrubs. Windows were opened and shut with incredible speed. Parasitic urban lianas were crawling up the willows around Botič Creek.

'Botič,' I said.

'Yeah, yeah, yeah, that's right,' my friend agreed. 'It's been recently cleaned or something. I remember when there were huge gobs of yellow foam floating on it, rusty tricycles standing in it, and the banks were overgrown. It used to be the Amazon of Nusle,[3] of sorts.'

In the bottom part of the steep little square was a gaping, local watering hole filled with smoke. Thick clusters of petiolated branches dangled on the sides of the steps.

'A Czech palm-tree for ya,' I said.

'Yes, yes, Tree of Heaven, I like it a lot,' my friend agreed. 'What appeals to me about it is that it's good-for-absolutely-nothing; even the Chinese who typically milk everything down to the very last drop leave it alone because it's completely useless – fragile timber, no fruit, nothing to devour, beautiful tree!'

'So, shall we?'

We climbed the brick stairs and peered inside. From the depths of a high-ceilinged room we heard the mumbling of several muted voices. An old man with large glasses on top of his nose was sitting alone at the longest table, regularly jerking his head, inspecting us reproachfully. He resembled a large, dusty fly. A wet stain was spreading on the ceiling, with water dripping from there into a bucket that had been placed below it.

'Great,' my friend responded lowering his voice. 'This is just like Svat˝ Jan pod skalou, the cave below the monastery. Have you ever been there?'

'Last summer,' I said. 'And you were there as well... and some women... and Dan Lima was there too.'

3. District of southern Prague

A waiter appeared as soon as we sat down.

'A Fernet for me,' I said out of habit, while at the same time realizing I'd actually quit drinking that liquor. Lately it had really become bad; it tasted of death and vile stomach chemicals. *Carefully selected herbs, traditional recipe and long maturation produce a unique amaro of exceptional flavour.* For twenty years this was true. But where do they keep getting those carefully selected herbs?

'One for me as well,' my friend said. 'Did you notice?' he leaned over to me after the waiter had left.

'Nope. Notice what?'

'Watch this!'

The server appeared in the passageway from the taproom. His rolled-up sleeves revealed two hands ending at the base of the palm. His beer-soaked stumps were holding a bright green tray with two shots of a dark liquid. He placed it at the table, put one glass in front of me, one in front of my friend. A part of each stump had a miniature dead thumb without a nail that looked like it had been assembled from the remains of a little finger.

'Two Fernets,' he said and left.

We watched him for a while as he moved briskly among the guests, bringing out beer, taking glasses away, and then reporting everything at the front of the room to a woman standing behind the tap, adding items to the bills of respective tables. His head was that of a handsome Central Bohemian, with his wavy hair combed back. He looked like someone who had earned a degree in physical education and happily married before it happened to him. Like the country's motorcycle speedway champ. Like Gabčík and Kubiš.[4] A golden-boy that any good mother would die for.

'I've always said that we'll live to the time when the world resembles a cartoon,' my friend stated.

'I'm not saying it's not so,' I said, 'but I think your view

4. Czech resistance fighters in WWII, killed after assassinating the occupying Nazi Governor, General Reinhard Heydrich, in 1942.

is largely the result of the way you spend your own private time...'

'How so?'

'Material gets worn out. Everything else stays the same, you just see it from a different point of view.'

'I'm not worn out,' my friend protested. 'Lately I've got nothing to complain about at all; everything's working just fine... Women – that's actually working better than ever, but there's no more *epiphany* there... I'm content with the mere memories of myself.'

'Sure, the less you belong in this world, the less obliged you feel to comment on it,' I said. And my uncertainty came back; am I an idiot or is he, that we always end up with such topics?

'But I still don't feel mentally crippled,' growled my friend, pricking his ears like a dog whose bowl is about to be taken away.

'Me neither, even if sometimes it looks that way from the outside,' I replied.

'Recently I went to pay my monthly phone bill, and I'm lining up before a cubicle with this little office Lolita in it, and when it's my turn I say: "Zero six zero three..." and that was it.'

'"Yes, and the rest?" she says. "Zero six zero three," I started, and again nothing else came. I just couldn't remember my own number that I'd been using for eight years. So I tried a couple more combinations, but they were all wrong! This, of course, got the attention of the people in line, and they were waiting to see what I'd do...'

'And what did you do?'

'Turned red and got out of there.'

'I know people who'd just fall apart then and there.'

'I'm not of such calibre yet.'

'But you cry during TV bedtime stories, don't you? I do after all these years...'

'I don't watch TV bedtime stories, but come Christmas

time when they show *Making Merry with Hellions,* I often struggle not to shed a tear...'

'Yeah. You really learn to deceive yourself through other people; everyone's taught this at primary school. Those teacher bitches coach you in that!'

'But do you think it's appropriate to spend the rest of your life with that as an excuse?' I replied in vain because this was one of his enduring topics.

'It hasn't really been discussed much!' he retorted in a perfectly harsh voice. 'The teachers who used to drill Russian into us should be shown in freak shows! Stupid cow maths teachers, they should be fed to feral P.E. teachers! Let them feel some freak show pain!'

'I don't perceive it that way because all I ever did during the first decade of my life was daydream and nothing could touch me.' I followed a worn-out path. 'And then you fall right into it of course: high-school, rock'n'roll, military service, broken hearts, plans and desires... But after struggling for all these years I'm finding now that, like it or not, I'm returning back to daydreaming.'

'Well, I salute you for that – that's how it should be!' My friend acknowledged my spiel and sipped from his glass. 'One should go out through the same door one came in! Oh yeah, aah, this is real gut-rot!'

'It is,' I agreed. 'Except I'm certainly not going out through any doors anytime soon. I just have no clue as to what I'm gonna do with myself for the next twenty years.'

'Things will happen, I'm not worried about that, as long as I have a clear head,' my friend continued. 'I don't mind being a gardener some place!'

'Eight hours a day? Can you imagine, spending the whole day with a lawnmower some place. It's dusty and hot... I'd really sooner be an editor...'

'A slumped-over coffee drinker whose spinal marrow is being sucked out by office vampires? You'd last about two weeks, staring into a screen, generating bullshit! You'd be bored out of your skull!'

'I know, but what I had in mind was some neat little publishing company.'

'Right, somewhere they're really dying to hire you just so they can change your adult nappies in the few years before you retire! I mean, how old are you? Forty-eight?'

'Forty four...'

'There you go! Besides, it's all the same everywhere – little magazines, kitchenettes, empty faces... Physical work's better! Clears your head!'

'Oh really? Overalls, lockers, sweaty bosses you have to smile at for a year, listening to them wank on about hockey, before they start paying attention to you?' I say. 'These self-important retards again? With their schedules hysterically over-packed so as not to ever catch a glimpse of how fucked up they really are? The same crap again? Like in the eighties?'

'No, not that again,' my friend conceded. 'Maybe just working independently.'

'But as what, since you can't do anything?'

'Well neither can you!'

'Yeah, neither can I...'

'It's true that, when I think about it, I just can't pretend I'm capable of taking it seriously,' he panted. 'You just can't go on spinning your wheels forever.'

'No, you can't.' I nodded. 'It feels like I'm living my tenth life at least. It's been so long since I found pleasure in wanking off over a poster of Suzi Quatro...'

'Really?' he perked up. 'Which one was that?'

'The short one, in leather.'

'Don't know her.'

'Blonde, but on the dark side.'

'I don't know her.'

'You must: plump, short, played bass!'

'Oh that one. A face-pulling clown!'

'She had a sweet little mug...'

'An idiot!'

'Maybe, but I thought she was cute.'

'I certainly didn't.'

'There's no way you'd think she was cute if you only like the types with legs starting right below their neck!' I countered.

'I like slender ones, all right. What can I do!'

'What can you do? There's nothing you can do about it!'

'Short little legs and huge arse – *that* I don't like...'

'Well it doesn't have to go that far for me either, but they do need to have a *shape*!' I said and felt a pang in my heart.

'Yeah, it's lovely when a chick's in the shape of a moon buggy and moves that way too!'

'I'm talking about *corresponding proportions*, you dickhead! I'm certainly not interested in a woman that resembles an enlarged stick insect!' I knocked back the remaining Fernet.

I peered over my friend's head onto the dusty bowels of the streets. After making sure I wasn't looking at him, he engaged in calmly observing his hands resting on the tablecloth. He'd been around the block and I'd been around the block, and we'd known each other a good fifteen years. I realized that we had quite possibly just reached the point after which we had nothing to say to each other. 'Bořivojova Street 13' floated through my mind. What's in Bořivojova Street 13? Where is Bořivojova Street 13? When was I there? Who lives at Bořivojova Street 13?

The handless waiter was making his way among the tables, his clammy paws skilfully balancing a tray with two oncoming snifters filled to the brim with the poisonous memory of something that used to be drinkable.

'We're doing all right anyway,' my friend said.

A flash of sunlight glowing through the antennas and wires and chimney-sweeps' footbridges blazed through the rusty liquid.

# Two Days in the
# Life of Eva F.

## Sandstone Rock Formation

'LET'S JUST GET ourselves over to that forked hump and we'll take a breather, OK?' panted Josef.

'Yep.' I nodded in agreement and watched a bird of prey circling right above our heads. It wasn't flapping its wings, just gliding, and you could clearly see it turning its head to see if there was anything it could snatch below it; peering round, pissed off. It was so quiet you could hear the pebbles crunching under our feet. A blanket of dust was rising up from the ground behind us. The wind carried it sideways.

'I'm thirsty,' I remarked to our feet. I didn't want to say it. But I did.

'We'll drink at the hump,' hawked Josef, and he had been right, we were stupid for dragging our arses up a hill in such a sweltering heat. Romantics.

'This place really reminds me of a trip I took with my dad once,' I bellowed.

'When?'

'When I was small... I told you already about how my father would always be taking me on trips, often getting up in the morning when it was still dark. We'd get to the train station, spend half the day travelling on the train – there was no holding him back – then we'd climb up some deserted ridge or get to a little lake among the reeds somewhere near Křivoklát Castle, and there we'd sit down; Dad would smoke a couple of his Start cigarettes, I'd have my Tatranka chocolate wafer, and then we'd be heading back to the station.'

'How old were you?'

'Maybe five... and one time we were in a peculiar landscape just like here, walking uphill all day, with pastures teeming with sheep and we just kept marching straight up as if heading to heaven. It really was a strange trip. I still don't know to this day if it wasn't a dream, because it looked like another world there...'

'So why didn't you ask him where it was?'

'I did, and not just the once, but he himself didn't remember exactly which places we'd been to because we did something different every week. He'd be shouting as soon as he got home in the evening: "Eva pumpkin, the Highlands are calling! Eva pumpkin äum äum äššumava...!" And then later on, when he was lying in bed at home with cancer, practically not recognizing anyone, a few days before he died he came-to and suddenly had these clear eyes. He looked around, turned to me, winked and said: "Howdy pumpkin, is that you? You and I have done some serious hiking haven't we, remember?" And I said yes and went out on the balcony to cry. And that was the last thing he ever said. He never woke up again.'

'You told me the last thing he ever said was: "All right girls, it's about time to pack it in!"'

'That he said to Mum, not me. I'd just gone out shopping.'

'Hm.'

We got to the top of the hill only to discover that this was by no means the end, because beyond it was the beginning of an unreal landscape full of such hills. We stared at a number of perpendicular cones – that looked like they'd been built by termites – holes and little valleys overgrown with dry shrubs. Some bluffs were so inclined and eroded from below, they looked as though they were ready to fall on their sides. Others were leaning on one another. Others still had boulders balancing on their tops. It looked like a gathering place of drastically enlarged plaster mushrooms and gnomes. We sat in the shade and had a drink of water that had become warm.

'We're in the dessert,' I exhaled.

'We certainly are,' responded Josef. 'I'm amazed at how well I know it here... this is exactly what my mental landscape looks like.'

'And where is your landscape located?'

'Here, here and here.' He pointed at his head, his heart and at the plastic bottle with the last of the water, which was resting on his lap.

'*Voilà*,' I said. And I became engrossed in observing how everything was gently glimmering before my eyes. The grains of metal or mica, or what have you, sharply glistening. We listened to the astounding silence for a while. Then we got up and began a gradual descent into the sandstone rock formation. We peered into cobwebbed shafts and crevices, climbed down strange, flat, horizontally cut boulders, pulled apart clumps of thistles and scared away long-legged spiders, which fled to safety with giant strides. Lizards would seamlessly disappear before us.

We discovered an entrance to a cave at the bottom of a mound. We climbed up to it over crumbling rubble, and gazed inside. Lying there at the bottom was a rolled-up blanket, a piece of foam, a few tins of sardines in oil and a bunch of empty paper packages printed with blue lettering. Above the foam was a shelf made from a plank, with several corked bottles surrounded by a limping multitude of teary candles. From behind them, a young man in a photo – his hair smoothed back, a tense look in his eyes, and wearing a tie – was watching us. A little black book with a crippled spine and dog ears lay in front of the picture. I picked it up and read:

*MOJSIJE DOBIVA OBDARENOST DA ČINI
ČUDA. POVRATAK U EGIPAT. A Mojsije
odgovori i reče: ali öati glasa mojega; jer ce reči: nije ti
se Gospondin javijo. A Gospodin mu reče: öta ti je to
u ruci? A on odgovori: ötap. A Bog mu reče: baci ga na
zemlju. I baci ga na zemlju, a on posta zmija. I Mojsi
pobjeûe od nje. A Gospodin reče Mojsiju: pruûi ruku
svoju, pa je uhvati za rep...*[5]

I got a whiff of the odour of mould and dust and glue
and flyspecks. A smell of something long-gone. I put the
book back in its place and picked up the photo. The man
had pouted fleshy lips and bushy animal-like eyebrows. Far
behind him was a Ferris wheel rising against the black and
white sky, packed with little rigidly sitting people, and there
was also a merry-go-round, some booths, and behind them
a building with a domed roof, part of an esplanade, and
another structure that resembles a plague column. Josef in
the meantime uncorked one of the bottles and was cautiously
sniffing it from a distance.

'A handsome man,' I said.

'Handsome but bad-tempered.'

'Why bad-tempered?'

'Because people with messed up nerves, choleric types
and such, often have jumbled eyebrows like that.'

'I see.' Then I speculated, 'What if it's the person who
lives here?'

'Then we should really split, in case he wants to give
you a little kiss with those harelipsssss, if he showed up...'
he said.

We slid down the grey rubble back to the shrubs, put

5. SIGNS FOR MOSES. Moses answered, 'What if they do not believe
me or listen to me and say, "The Lord did not appear to you"?' Then the
Lord said to him, 'What is that in your hand?' 'A staff,' he replied. The
Lord said, 'Throw it on the ground.' Moses threw it on the ground and it
became a snake, and he ran from it. Then the Lord said to him, 'Reach out
your hand and take it by the tail.'

on our backpacks and carried on. Slowly we began to feel that we just weren't able to get ourselves out of this no man's land and that we were going in circles. That we were passing places we'd been to at least once before. But then we found ourselves walking on a narrow concrete path assembled from broken paving slabs.

We'd barely walked a few metres before an old man on a bicycle appeared from behind a curve, dressed in a thick, solid jacket – it may have been about forty degrees – and with his head lost in a broad flat cap with a brim. He was slowly peddling towards us. The gears were squeaking. A filthy cloth bag was dangling from the handlebars.

'Pardon me, Vaganski Vrh?[6] Which way?' Josef enunciated.

The guy looked up, saw us, waggled his handlebars, and while still riding, he and his boneshaker keeled over onto the path. As he fell, a cracking sound came from the bag and a thick reddish liquid started pouring out. He remained on the ground.

'Holy fuck!' Josef said in fright.

The man was looking at us from the ground, moving his stubble-covered chin. A dark puddle was quickly spreading on the concrete. A nagging, sour smell reached us – some preserved fruit or a marmalade.

'What are we gonna do?' I blurted out.

'Just don't panic, all right, I'll help him,' said Josef and tried to help the man back on his feet. The geezer was still straddling the frame of his bike. Josef was pulling, trying to pick him up together with his old clunker. The geezer slipped out from his grasp, slowly rolled over, sat up and carefully put on his gigantic hat. He was looking at us like we were apparitions. He got up, grabbed the handlebars which Josef handed over to him and gradually put his leg over the crossbar. He was wearing a pair of old shoes with cut off heels, showing the pitch black heels of his bare feet.

6. Vaganski Pike

'Vaganski Vrh?' Josef tried again, overemphasizing the second syllable.

'Vaganski Vrh – da, tam!'[7] the geezer gestured with his liver-spot covered hand and the fork of his bike began to waver dangerously again but the geezer more or less balanced it out and continued on his journey. We watched him until he disappeared. Then we turned our heads in the direction he'd pointed us in. We discovered that there was another steep hill covered in a skimpy, sparse forest, rising directly above the sandstone rock formation.

We finished walking the last bit of the way, which suddenly seemed comfortable and alluring because it was straight. Behind the last cliff, the path split, with one route climbing the stoney hillside. We took it. After a while I noticed the bird of prey circling above us again. It looked like the same one. Wind currents were ruffling the feathers on its neck. Apparently it still hadn't found anything to snatch. We passed among the orange trunks of pine trees emanating an intoxicating smell. The view on the other side opened itself up before us.

## A Change of Pace

The real mountain, the one we had intended to climb, was glowing blue, high above us, and had two peaks. The higher one was further away. It was my idea to climb it. It was Josef who said this could take ages. We were running out of water. All we'd had to eat were a few biscuits and a melted chocolate bar. It was our second day of going up and up. We spent the first night in a dilapidated lodge that hadn't seen any guests in years. Our car was somewhere down in the valley, parked by a little church. It was being guarded for a handful of change. Perhaps right now, someone was taking off one of the wheels. Josef was silent.

7. Vaganski Pike – yes, over there!

'So are we climbing up there?' I asked.

'Most certainly, since we're here already. Don't you want to?'

It was a scorcher. I didn't have the slightest inclination to do it. We'd thought we were taking off for a one-day trip. But it just wouldn't do to simply turn around and head back the same way.

'Sure I do.'

A sharply defined cloud was slowly making its way across the sky.

'That cloud over there resembles a hand, look, one directing us to go back,' I said.

I was watching Josef's legs – in faded black shorts – marching before me. I knew exactly what he was thinking. That I talk too much. That I have to blurt out whatever comes to mind. That it sometimes is unbearable. The air around us trembled like pudding being cooked. It didn't want to go into the lungs at all.

'It's strange, anyway...' I puffed.

'What is?'

'What we're doing here.'

'The present is always strange.'

'What is the present?'

'What we're doing here, no?'

'Hm.'

'You don't like it?' came at me from ahead.

'I'm not sure I like the fact that we've been scrambling uphill for two days till we're blue in the face.' – I stoked the fire.

'That's right, that's what we're doing,' admitted Josef.

'But why?'

'Because that's what we wanted. What does everyone in the world want, Eva?' he uttered towards the hillside.

'Hey Shiva Shankara, I don't have a clue.'

'Well, give it some thought.'

I did. To live. To have children. To be happy. Healthy.

To have money. To have affairs. To humiliate just about anyone. To come up with even more disgusting filth.

'To get something they don't yet have, right?' is what occurred to me, like I was in grade eight. 'So they can check it off their list and want something else...'

'Exactly,' he growled.

This is what I loved about him; he was able to gently remind me of what I had already known myself.

'The present,' mused Josef. 'The present is a never-ending attempt to play the same song – a song that's always been played the same way – only better this time. It's nothing but a mere remix...'

Remix, remix, remix, clicked a metronome in my head. *He's* always got to be the smarter one. But if it weren't him, it would have to be me. Which, as I know from experience, is quite shitty.

'You know why I love you, Josef?'

'Because I'm your Wailing Wall,' he replied without hesitation.

Actually yes. In fact, that's it. He hit the nail on the head.

'No, you're not,' I said.

'Yes I am,' he confirmed to himself, perhaps feeling a little frightened by the thought.

Gravel crunched underneath our feet.

'We really should have gone to Amsterdam instead,' I added unnecessarily. 'We'd be having a smoke somewhere in the shade, watching people, cruising the canals and chatting, sipping coffee... Shit, I'd love a cup of coffee!'

'Hm,' came his voice, from in front of me.

'Or just a slice!' I hankered. 'Just a thin slice!'

'A slice of what?' he couldn't help himself.

'Anything.'

I heard him chuckle.

'And instead we travel to such a barren shithole!' I started up again.

'Amsterdam is a thoroughly stupid city,' objected Josef.

'Maybe in a few years there won't be any Amsterdam,' I say. 'Swoosh and the water takes it away...'

'No great loss.'

'And all the Dutch will move to the Jizera Mountains and grow tulips...'

'Better than Praguers who go there twice a month to read tabloids and guzzle Becherovka.'

'You know the Dutch have already been moving to the Jizeras, did you know that? They've been buying land there...?'

'I've heard about it.'

The gravel became loose with every step and rolled away. The hills around us were covered in thin grass, laced with meandering white paths, even though it was unclear who'd ever be walking there or why.

'I wouldn't be surprised to see the Marlboro Man ride right past us,' commented Josef.

The gravel kept tumbling far below us, bouncing off rocks and dislodging more stones as it went. You couldn't take a single step without causing a landslide.

'Look up and tell me, is that an eagle?' I asked.

'Where?'

'The one that keeps circling above us... Is that an eagle?'

We looked up. An empty, unfathomable sky was vibrating above us. Nothing there.

'Sure, the eagle of the rock,' he teased.

The grit rattled and clattered in dry little voices. It was lamenting, like souls in hell. I stopped looking down below my feet and peered into eternity, a bit above the horizon. I realized that with each stride and breath, a delicate new veil descended over my mind. But they weren't fogging up my brain; on the contrary, I felt all the blockage dissolving from it. Preconceptions. My mouth was still yammering but my soul felt almost at peace.

'I haven't felt this peaceful in years,' I said.

'That's the change in rhythm... When was the last time you spent two days hiking uphill?'

True, it had been a long time.

From the shimmering air the mountain peak gradually emerged before us.

I farted.

Josef burst out laughing like a madman.


## Vaganski Vrh

We heard jingling. A herd of sheep was pouring down a hillside before us and a man covered head to toe in a shaggy blanket was bouncing along behind it. He was waving at us with his stick and, even from this distance, shouting something at us. He was walking sort of askew as if one of his legs were shorter. The closer he got, the louder he yammered.

'Kokite, kakite tete!' he shouted.

'Vratite se!' we heard when he came closer. 'Vratite se! Kamo idete?!'[8]

'Vaganski vrh,' said Josef.

'Ne, ne!' he shook his perpendicular stick at us. 'Idite natrag! Curyk! Curyk! Nazad!'[9]

'That's our business,' we objected.

'Éé!' he pierced the air all around with his stick. 'Éé! Svuda na okolo su mine! Mine! Achtung minen! Bum! Izgubit cete nogu?' his arms flailed. 'Boommm! Verstehen si? Nemáte cigaretu? Zigarette?'[10]

We gave him half a pack. For that he rewarded us

8. 'Come back!'... 'Come back! Where are you going?!'
9. 'No, no'... 'Get back! Zurück! Zurück! Get back!'
10. 'Hey!'... 'Hey! There are mines everywhere! Mines! Attention Mines! Boom! Wanna lose a leg?'... 'Boooom! Understand? Have you got a cigarette?

with another extended speech during which he repeated everything several times. We assured him we'd go down. That we'd take a rest and go back the same way. That we were from the Czech Republic. That things were all right there. But that his country was more beautiful. Except for the mines. He chuckled. Foul breath wafted from his mouth, he lit a cigarette, shook his calloused hand with us several times and went on his way. The sheep poured over a ridge and disappeared. The jingling faded away on the other side of the hill. We sat down in the grass right beside the path. I took my bandanna off and twirled it between my fingers. Josef was watching me from the side.

'So what do you think?' he queried.

'To hell with it, let's keep going.' I waved my hand. He caressed my hair. Put it behind my ears. Tied my bandana on me. And he kissed me through it on the top of my head.

We got up and carried on. We followed the path but slowed down quite a bit. Strangely, our fatigue was suddenly gone. We were ascending the steep landscape. Every step brought us a bit higher. The world lay below us like an unlikely garden from a Dutch painting captured in the most painstaking detail. There were rolling valleys and sprawling plains. Billions of the same old petty events taking place down there. There were crawling trains. Children were being put to sleep. Newspapers leafed through. People loafed around their TV-sets. *And a panty-liner*, the walls echoed, *oh, I've already got one!* Folks looking out of their open windows, flicking ash into the wind, and the hospitals and swimming pools and movie theatres and refrigeration plants and jails were operating at full tilt. A little hobbling figure was mushroom-picking in a tiny grove, lost outside the city. A jay rustled in the branches, blinked its dopey eye and let out a cry; a little figure paused, and looked around. At the other end of the grove a different little man was raping a little woman, giving her angry little slaps in the face to shut her up as she uttered freaky groans. A white bum was shining under the trees like a coin. A cone fell off a tree into the moss. It was rolling. Europe lay there as if on a plate. Beyond Europe there was a flickering ocean studded with ships. There were bored sailors on those ships. Death hunkered on a tree by the road, holding an hourglass in its chicken talons, waiting for the knight.

'Listen, Josef...' I said.

'Don't you worry,' he answered. 'We'll be careful... Why turn back now? We've got to spend the night here anyhow. It's a good thing I thought of bringing along the sleeping bags.'

'Wasn't that my idea?'

'All right, good thing you thought of bringing along the sleeping bags.' He put his arms around my shoulders.

That was what I found so attractive about him. His calmness. But it was also what made me so jealous.

The woodland limped towards us. A pink light exploded around us, spilling over the sky like mercury, wrapping us in purple shadows. I wanted to say that I'd never seen a colour like this. I wanted to say that these were royal colours. That I was feeling like St. George's maiden. Like a maiden watching the veins of the dragon pulse through his blood-filled scrag. That I was feeling like a fly trapped in a kaleidoscope.

'Fuck me if I ever saw a colour like this before,' commented Josef.

A gigantic, bare peak rose above the treetops, lit by the remains of the sunlight. We walked into the woods. After a few steps, a plateau opened up before us, partitioned by a low, dry-stone wall. We schlepped ourselves over to it, undid the straps of our backpacks, ditched them and threw ourselves on the ground. We unpacked our sleeping bags and rolled over onto them. For a long time we just lay there looking up.

I felt something tickling me. A black ant was crawling

on my calf. There wouldn't have been anything out of the ordinary about it had it not been five times bigger than any other ant I'd ever seen. I picked a blade of grass and held it to my leg. The ant transferred onto it, painstakingly dragged itself up and halted at the end. I took a close look at it and beheld a horribly callous armour-plated face. Eyes popping out of a flat, solid mask with interlocking mandibles underneath. I had a feeling it had noticed me. That it was staring at me. Its mandibles opened somewhat. It looked as if it was trying to say something.

'How can something like this exist, here, along with us?' I marvelled. 'Something so... different?'

'They could say exactly the same thing about you.'

I flicked the ant off into a plastic cup and lit a cigarette. It promenaded around like it was in an arena. There were a few regular little red ants scrabbling in the sand. Some were dragging eggs. Those I left alone. I picked about ten of those not carrying anything and put them with our strapping lad. They twirled their antennae and instantly attacked him. The armoured bug sped-up, circling around for a while, as the mandibles of the red ones sunk into its body. Then it fell on its side and began to twitch hopelessly.

'Come on, Eva!' murmured Josef.

I tossed the contents of the cup onto the grass.

Josef put his hand into my sleeping bag.

'Careful, I got sunburn,' I said.

His fingers travelled along my spine. Up as if on stairs and down as if on stairs. They began to scratch me between my shoulder-blades. They cautiously explored how things were coming along in my neck area. Then they changed their mind and went downwards. They walked all the way to the edge of my undies. In that moment I thought of the giant ant for some reason. The index finger slid under the elastic, pulled it out and let go.

'It's unhealthy,' he said and pulled them off.

'It's not healthy,' I agreed and pulled off his boxer

shorts.

The locusts were making our ears buzz with their screeching.

'Oh,' I breathed to the stars.

## Vaganski Vrh – The Night

I was lying in an unzipped sleeping bag watching the Moon.

'I've never seen the Moon this huge, is that even possible?' I said.

'Me neither... It's got the face of Karel Hála.'

'Who?'

'*He-llo Ma-jor Ga-ga-rin,*' he hummed.

'Dunno, who's that?'

'You're young.'

I stared up in silence. Josef was silent as well.

'If you drop a kilo weight and a pigeon's feather on the Moon, they'll both fall at the same speed and hit the ground at the same time,' he said.

'How'd you know that?'

'Scott, the astronaut tested it after landing there.'

'So he brought along a kilo weight and a pigeon's feather with him just for that?'

'Apparently.'

'The weight won't hit the ground even a tenth of a second sooner?'

'Nope.'

'You know Josef, you're not my Wailing Wall,' I said. 'At least not just that. You know why I really love you?'

'Why you really love me? I don't know,' he yawned.

'Oh, never mind, you're yawning... Go to sleep.'

'Don't be getting offended,' he yawned. 'You don't need to have every single impulse under control... Just rest a bit!'

'How am I supposed to be resting with this thing floating above us? How can it be so huge?'

'Well, you knoow... it's distorted by the aaawtmosphere... aaaha... aaawgh... Arghchr... chrr... zzzz,' he answered.

I lay in my sleeping bag watching the Moon. It was rolling low above us like a flying island. It was descending towards the mountain and looked as if it was about to crash into it. That it would squish us into the ground with its shiny belly. The locusts fell silent at once. Some small swift animal slid through the grass. A moth dashed right above the ground. I felt the flutter of its wings on my forehead. I shuddered. Josef was snoozing away. Some bird screeched nearby, and it sounded more like someone was blowing their nose. The plateau suddenly appeared small to me. I leaned over to get a cigarette out of my backpack. I froze in the middle of the motion.

Two faces were glowing in the dark behind the dry-stone wall. They stared and didn't move. At first I thought I was just imagining things out of fatigue. Very slowly I pulled my arm back. I shook my head to make the image go away. The faces started to shift uneasily and moved a bit further away. My heart began to thump. Those mugs kept watching us and slowly, ever so slowly, came back a bit closer. They looked like the made-up faces of clowns. Like two ham actors. There were empty smiles, curious crooked frowns and the occasional inquisitive cock of the head. I closed my eyes. When I opened them again, I saw it even more clearly: those two pancakes were silently laughing at us.

My eyes then glided down to the bottom of the meadow and I gasped: a towering white figure was standing there, tall and skinny. It was standing there and had no face, or maybe it did, but I was too afraid to even imagine what it might look like. Sheer terror emanated from that corner of the meadow.

It hesitated. Walked back and forth. Then it started towards us. I felt my arse contracting out of fear. And I could not take a breath. I was cold. It was coming towards us, and that was no coincidence, it *intended* to approach us. Then it stopped. It stood there swaying. As if it had reached an invisible barrier. As if it was considering how to continue. Stay here, I heard a voice ringing in my own head, don't go away! Stay here, I begged the two. Suddenly I grasped everything, or at least some of it. I felt as if someone had just let out an anxious howl at the top of their lungs inside of me. But the reality remained the same. Two semi-translucent mugs were staring at us while the dreadful spook crept around behind them.

I slowly turned my head.

'Josef,' I breathed into his ear.

'What is it?' he whimpered.

'Let's get outta here, please...'

'What?'

'Let's... get outta here...'

'What the...? Why? Where?'

'Someone's staring at us...'

'Where?'

'Over there.'

He turned his head.

'That's all right,' he grumbled, 'It's just some animals,' and he fell asleep again.

I pulled my head back into the sleeping bag and left only a tiny hole for breathing. Fine, let's croak here. We shouldn't have come here anyway. We'll just croak here and that's that. I'm not looking. My heart was no longer thumping, just tingling. And while holed in, I felt even more intensely that something really was out there. That it was aware of us. And it *wanted* something from us. That it wanted *us*. Life is nothing but agony from the start, it was saying. A long one, incredibly long. It wasn't saying it, just thinking it. Actually, it was me thinking about it. But I don't wanna die! Oh God, give me just a little more time!

Finally I couldn't stand it anymore and looked out

again. The phantoms were chuckling at me rudely. If it were just the two, I'd even try talking to them. Except there was something unspeakable fluttering behind them to the left. This was visceral, slimy fear. I couldn't resist not looking any longer and focused in on it. *Brrrrrr!* went my soul.

## Guests

Even before opening my eyes I realized I was drenched in sweat. The midmorning swelter was baking our sleeping bags. I unzipped my sleeping bag and sat up. My eyes turned to the wall. I recalled everything again. I lay on my back and tried to make some sense of things. It was not a dream. They were not humans either. So what was it? How come I fell asleep at all? Perhaps out of exhaustion. And out of fear. And here we are again. Alive.

'Josef?' I tossed the name in the air and it sounded as if spoken under water.

'Yeah...'

'Did you see that, last night?'

'I was completely wiped,' he responded. 'But I did catch a glimpse...'

'Of what?'

'Down there, probably stray sheep... and there was some, someone... some woman...'

'And you're telling this to me just like that? How could you just fall asleep and leave me here with that?'

'I thought it was just a dream.'

'But I woke you up because of it!'

'You're needlessly oversensitive!'

That certainly cannot be ruled out. We packed our sleeping bags, going through the familiar steps, and stuffed them into our backpacks, gulped a few drops of water, and left the clearing.

The main peak of the mountain rose directly above us.

We were separated from it by only a shallow bowl, and then there was but constant ascent.

'How're you doin'?' asked Josef.

'We've got almost nothing to drink,' I said.

'We'll be there in three hours...'

'I know.'

'You've had enough, haven't you?'

'Yeah,' I admitted.

We headed to the bowl and didn't take another look at the mountain. A wide, bare, rocky pass opened up under our feet. We went down, walking around the rocks without a single word. The sun was behind us and the light shone past us down into the valley, and our shadows bounced on the cliffs like disgustingly thin mantises.

A hut clinging to the hillside with a roof of warped slabs — a log house of sorts — appeared behind the curve. Smoke was coming out of the metal pipe sticking out of the roof in place of a chimney, despite the morning heat. We automatically headed there and knocked on the door. Something which sounded like 'Hi-der!' came from inside. We entered. In the middle of the dark, wooden room, and under a cloud of smoke, about eight men sat around a table with sets of worn out cards in their hands. They were looking us up and down with their yellowed eyes.

'Hello,' we said.

Two or three of them nodded and gestured to us to sit down. We leaned our backpacks against the foot of the table and sat down.

'Ehm, hm,' Josef began the conversation.

No one responded. Broken up branches burned in the fireplace where a large pot hung over the flames, not moving. A cow's skull with horns sticking out dangled on the wall. The room was as hot as a furnace. The cards were slapped against the table. Two icons, one red, one greenish white, both in silver frames, glowed dimly from the corner of the room. Only after a while did I realize that these were no icons but rather Samantha Fox, a tits and arse trollop with an empty face, ripped out of a magazine and fitted into a frame wrapped in tin foil, painstakingly smoothed out. The second picture showed a good-natured, skinny woman with a crooked smile and a garish green wig with two greased German cocks inside her and holding two others – each at one of her ears – as if she was about to find out something interesting from them.

An unbelievably wide bald-headed old man was sitting on a bench back by the wall, staring at us without blinking. There was something growing from underneath his bulbous nose that covered the entire lower half of his face. It looked like he was holding a broom in his teeth or something. Some kind of oakum. Or perhaps, I thought with alarm, some animal that had bitten him got stuck there. Gradually I realized that it had to be a moustache.

'Šta tu radite?'[11] moved the whiskers.

'Tourists,' we answered, using that hideous but recognizable word.

'I odkuda idete?'[12]

'Vaganski Vrh,' we answered.

The old man kept peering at us with his eyes framed by black-purple circles.

'To nije moguče![13] *This* is Vaganski Vrh!' he declaimed in a voice that was obviously not used to any opposition, wheezing through his nose at the same time.

'But we're coming from the second hill,' we said.

'Now? In the morning?'

'We spent the night there.'

'You spent the night there?' he echoed.

The wood in the fireplace crackled and the flame tossed up a pile of sparks around the pot.

11. 'What are you doing here?'
12. 'And where are you coming from?'
13. 'That's not possible!'

A shorter, young man with an obnoxiously thick neck and a negligible head in proportion to it got up from the table and fixed his gaze on us. 'You...!' he skewered us with his index finger. 'You come around here to our country and don't know shit about what you should and shouldn't do! You don't know that you don't sleep over there...? That nobody lives there...? That vipers fall from trees right onto your neck over there? That you die from a snake bite in a minute...? That only ghosts live there...?! You don't know a thing, do you! You just gawk! You gawk and that's it! All you want to do is gawk!'

We didn't understand him but grasped very well what was on his mind.

'What do you want from us?' he repeated. 'Why do you come to our land! Why don't you just stay where you came from, Jesus fucking Christ, fuck your Ei-Eiffel Tower, fuck your stupid country! What the fuck do you know about how we live here, huh! What the fuck do you know about what one man can do to another, huh! Why the fuck do you come here, huh!'

His head had been battered and scarred like a concrete milestone. He was gesturing and coming closer to us. He was speaking and spattering and gasping.

'Why do you prance around here with your bride!' he focused on Josef and spattered all over him. 'Why do you come to us! Why don't you take her away while you can! You're our guests, we wo-won't hurt you, eat and drink! And th-th-then ggg... then gggo away! Zašto o-o-ovdûe v-v-vrljudaš sa svojom cu-curom! äta?!'[14]

'Quiet!' the patriarch thundered from the corner.

The younger man turned around, shifting his whole body like a ram, and headed for the bench, but the old man stopped him and quickly gave him several orders. The dwarf marched to the fire place where he took some things off,

14. 'Why are you w-w-wandering around h-h-here with your girlfriend! What?!'

put something else in and then placed a tin bowl filled with mushy matter resembling shredded apple and carrots, but smelling of garlic and meat before us. He placed a couple of grubby flatbreads and a few tomatoes by the bowl, made a jerking move with his forehead as if to bow, averted his eyes and returned to his place. We grabbed our spoons. It was ground meat with some squash. It tasted a bit of rancid suet and desolation, but starving as we were, we wolfed it down. The men looked on. I noticed one wearing a freshly ironed shirt and a camouflage military hat pushed to the back of his neck. There was something about him I found disturbing; perhaps the fact that he had a small, pink, selfish, child-like mouth even though his hair was already grey. That he looked like an aged spoiled hunk not used to denying himself anything. A bit like a cross-dressed woman. He was gazing at us with his turquoise eyes and didn't blink once. Occasionally he chimed in a few words, and the others briefly laughed. The room was filling up with smoke.

## Ubil si ju![15]

While we were finishing our meal, the unsightly young man with a scarred head brought in a demijohn. He put out glasses and poured yellow wine into them, spilling some on the table. We put our bowls away and thanked them for the meal. A loud squeak came from the wall. The old man got up and with difficulty walked over to the table. He seized a glass.

'To our health, to our children's and your children's health and to their children's health!' he declared solemnly. 'That you may be happy, and that your children may also be happy! Uûivaj ûivot sa ûenou koju ljubiš, i u dobro vrijeme uûivaj dobro, i u zlo hvali Gospodina...,'[16] he said, 'nek sa

15. 'You killed her!'
16. 'Enjoy life with your wife, whom you love and when times are good, be happy and when they are bad, praise the Lord...'

veselite... i nek sa radujete... i kaka... i ovaka... i ûelim da budete kod u nas zadovolnji!'[17]

Everyone nodded in agreement, turned to look at us and waited.

'When I went to see Manda, I fell in a pit / I was still lucky though, that I was wearing no shoes. / If I'd been wearing boots, / I wouldn't be in cahoots; / I'd have poor Manda now, singing the blues,' chanted Josef. 'We love this place, / you've got nice weather and people with grace. / We got Charles Bridge / and you... plenty of wine and sausage, / I'm a Slav, you're a Slav, my mother's from Davle and the old man from Pribyslav. / So raise the chalice and have no malice. / Hail "Hallelujah, long may we live!"'

The men listened intently. The old man contentedly clenched his teeth, held up his moustache with his hand and pushed his glass underneath it. We drank, finished it and the dwarf again refilled everyone's glass.

'What was that gobbledygook you came up with?' I asked after a bit.

'I have no idea,' answered Josef.

The wine was sour. I could feel the alcohol go straight to my heart after all that. At least it helped to get the conversation going a bit. How are things in your country, and yours? What about politics? We chatted. My answers were mumbled and while I kept a smile on my face, I was slowly feeling overcome by total fatigue after all we'd been through.

'Ere we like blondes the best,' the men changed the topic. 'A blonde woman's gotta become a theatre actress! She just dances and sings, you know, no need to work, just sing! We're really wild for blondes!'

'It doesn't matter so much for us,' Josef responded, 'as long as the woman's good-hearted!'

'When she does as she's told, right? She's got to do as

17. 'May you be happy... and may you rejoice... and this... and that... and I want you to be content here with us!'

she's told, ain't that right?'

'For sure,' said Josef.

'And what about your bride, does she do as you tell her?'

'Sometimes,' Josef was trying to deflect the subject.

'As long as you don't do as she tells you!' laughed the blue-eyed one wearing the camouflage hat. But his eyes were cold.

Josef shrugged.

'And is she your bride at all? Will you be getting married?' they enquired.

Josef nodded and it was clear that he was getting pissed off while being aware that this would be the least pertinent thing to do in our situation.

'And what kinda hair does your bride have? Why won't she show it to us?' asked the blue-eyed one, sucking air in between his teeth and smacking his lips grotesquely.

'That's right... Why doesn't your bride take off her kerchief! Just for a second' the others joined in and laughed, showing their teeth, but their eyes were suddenly different.

'We're not gonna gobble her up!' said the blue-eyed one and produced another strange smack.

'We're just gonna check a little what sort of a bride you got!'

The brain in my head just did not feel like responding. But after watching Josef cocking his ears, I had to admit to myself that that there was something off. I noticed him touching the pouch on his backpack where his knife was stored. But what good is a knife with eight sloshed guys sitting around and staring at me, plus it was obvious that while they themselves were not quite sure yet what was going through their minds, we'd need to reckon with it as soon as they figured it out. I'd never been a blonde in my entire life, but that was beside the point.

I couldn't take my thoughts any further than that because the blue-eyed one got up, bent over a chest, pulled out a rifle and put it on the table. It was so unexpected it didn't even frighten me.

'So. Can you shoot?' he asked Josef.

'I can,' answered Josef.

'You can shoot? A Czech?'

'I can,' insisted Josef.

'Let's see,' said the man and poured a bunch of chiming opaque cartridges on the table. Then he very quickly said something to the dwarf. He pulled out a chair and took the cow's skull down from the wall. I spotted two rows of coarse blackened teeth underneath the sharp, long, nose bones. It occurred to me that it was as if the cow had not been produced by nature but H. R. Giger instead. The dwarf turned his whole body to us since he was apparently unable to turn his head and he held the skull in his arms. The man in the hat gave him an order in a voice now surprisingly high and unpleasantly sharp. The dwarf ran outside with the skull, and the guy in the hat directed him through an open window – put it there, not there! Further away! I leaned over and peered outside. The skull was stuck in a tree on the hillside far from the log house. The man took a look at Josef and handed him the weapon. It was dark and faded.

'If you hit the mark, we'll drink wine and sing; if not – your bride will show us what kinda hair she's got,' he said.

'That's out of the question,' said Josef, now quite harshly.

'You don't understand what I'm saying? If you miss, we'll keep your bride here with us and you go for a walk! We got some gorgeous scenery, you'll take a walk and come back in two hours!'

They all laughed. For the second time that day already, I tasted the dry metallic taste of fear in my mouth. I fixed my gaze on the old man with the moustache looking for some solution or at least an explanation from him, but he kept looking in the distance seeming to approve of everything – why not let the young ones have some fun? – or else his thoughts were wandering who knows where.

Josef took the rifle. I saw him quickly examine how to work everything, then he picked up a cartridge, clicked the lever, inserted it and closed it shut as if this was something he did every day. He raised the rifle and aimed it out into the light. I saw it dip at first as it was perhaps heavier than he had expected. There was dead silence.

Then came a deafening bang. An unusually strong smell of gunpowder hit me over the nose.

Everyone rushed to the window.

'Oj! Oj! D-dobro!'[18] shouted the dwarf, shuddering and gasping with excitement.

'The cow is dead!' the Yugos yelled and laughed.

'Ubil si ju!'[19] the old man stated contentedly.

I looked out. The nose bones were gone, replaced by a jagged hole in the head. Then others joined in; they passed the rifle to one another and kept shooting again and again till the bones had completely shattered apart. The gun made its way back to Josef, and I could see that he was getting into it. That they had all but forgotten about me. And that in this moment I wasn't really there in his mind either. He managed to shoot off a horn. The dwarf hooted with excitement, beating his chest with the palm of his hand, shuffling his feet, rubbing his hands and sputtering white saliva.

I covered my ears and waited for them to wrap it up. Afterwards, there was more drinking. Josef was now their man. They always filled his glass first. Then mine. Then theirs. Then more toasts were proposed. They would wink at me for having such a fine man. We would tell them something and they would burst out laughing and slapping their thighs and then frown and nod with concern. During our discourse we sang for them *Before the dawn, the Captain gives orders, spurring the horse before he's gone...*

The guys were all ears, swaying with rhythm, humming with us: *Imaš vina, krčmaricu, zabavljat ćemo se cijelu no?!*[20]

The dwarf's excitement got out of hand. In his glee

18. 'G-Good!'
19. 'You killed her!'
20. 'You got wine, a sulteress, we'll have a merry old time all night long!'

he grabbed the rifle, turned around with it, and aimed at everyone. He then focused on me and Josef, aimed at us, clicking his teeth, grimacing while countless wrinkles puckered up his pug-dog forehead. 'Bam!' he yelped at us. But since everyone was laughing heartily, I figured it couldn't be as dangerous as it seemed. At last he put the rifle's barrel in his mouth pretending this time to shoot himself for a change, 'bam, bam!' he muttered, his gullet heaving, and he giggled with delight while simultaneously checking with a frantic, dreary eye that we were laughing sufficiently at his number.

The sun rolled over the roof and the fire died out. We announced that we had to be going. 'If you gotta go, you gotta go,' they said. The dwarf pleaded with us to stay. He grabbed at our arms. He knelt in front of us. 'Why don't you st-stay, it's all right up h-hhere! It's not all right down th-there, here it is!' he begged. 'We'll eat and drink and s-sing! We'll dance! Grab a g-guitar!'

We found ourselves outside again, saddled with our backpacks. The dwarf kept leaping around us, fidgeting, scratching himself, cracking his fingers and howling. 'K-kyrie eleison!'[21] he barked after us. He looked longingly in our direction for a long time. Only when it was clear that we wouldn't be coming back did he return to his people.

## K-kyrie Eleison!

Our knees were hurting from our swift descent down the mountainside. The valley would drop down away from our feet left and right. Tiny, bristly purple flowers cropped out of the cracks and crevices. Just a few in some places, and entire islands bursting just around the bend. Soft tussocks of hair-grass a bit further down started to brush against our calves and clouds of little flies swarmed out of them and took an

21. 'Lord have mercy.'

interest in us. We slapped our legs and faces.

'I had no idea you could shoot,' I said, my teeth chattering.

'Me neither.'

A dilapidated little church with a wooden roof appeared behind a limestone cliff. It was nesting on the hillside, the whole thing leaning to one side, holding on for dear life. A grass covered branch of the path we were going down wound towards it. We went down to the church and peered inside, through windows that were no more than a foot wide. We felt a waft of dark, musty air.

'Oh-la-la, my friend, it's early Gothic.' Josef patted the rugged moss-covered wall built from rough hewn rocks, 'but how did it come to be up here in the hills?'

The make-shift door, patched together from planks, had been pushed in, and its frame was so low that we had to take off our backpacks and bend down quite a bit to get in. The space we entered was notably smaller than it appeared from the outside. It was cold inside. Painfully bright streaks of light cut in through narrow embrasures. When I stepped into one of them, I felt as if I was under an X-ray machine. As if all my bones could be seen. We walked around the space, examining the walls and both, in our own way, pulling ourselves together. A low, plastered table shone white by the back wall. I went to take a look. There were some faded doodles on the wall behind it.

'That's strange,' said Josef sniffing the plaster close up, 'strange, strange... This could only be an altar, but how old? Six hundred years easily.'

I looked on, as he took a close look at the doodles behind the altar. After my eyes had adjusted to the darkness, I made out two suns of equal size on the wall. One was black and the other white and both were so faint that they must have been there a very long time. A stone relief jutted out of the wall between them. It was a naked body with short legs lying in a fetal position with its arms crossed, apparently a dead villager. He looked a bit like a run-over dog. His mouth was wide open. A crucifix protruded from it. On the crucifix was a sinewy figure with a prematurely aged, worn-out face. Untimely, cruel wrinkles had been carved into his forehead. He was the height of a year-old baby, carved out of a soft grey stone smoothed out and greasy as if generation after generation of widows had been coming here to caress him and ask for forgiveness. In a moment when Josef was not looking, I slid my finger over the crucified man's ribs. I touched his knee and his stomach and felt his icy, salamandrine skin. As if I had touched a mummy. It made my stomach a bit queasy, so I tried focusing my attention on the two suns instead. The white one looked like a chunk of melted suet and was frowning away, while the black one was spreading its dim mouth into a wide unconvincing smile.

'That's strange all right,' I exhaled.

'Not really,' Josef responded. 'In the twelfth and thirteenth centuries it was a common theme when a Christian got involved with a pagan. These suns used to crop up in our neck of the woods as well, but they have been covered up or destroyed for the most part, since the symbolism they exude is a little too obvious...'

'The world is a horrible place,' I shuddered.

'But in an interesting way.' He was rejoicing, now he was safely in his element – *The Golden Bough, The Secret History of Europe, Forbidden Archaeology*.

'Cause it's basically purely pagan symbolism,' he explained. 'A man and a woman, the heaven and the Earth, the dance of opposites... Sometime they were even understood as symbolizing succubus and incubus, but not much is known about it nowadays.'

That was his element. One time we were lying in bed and in classic fashion I asked him, 'What are you reading?' and Josef showed me the flap of one of his secret histories, and there was a photo of the author instantly revealing a condescending, bleating moron with a beard and shifty eyes – we had one look at him and started to laugh like mad, because it was so apparent – but only a minute later, Josef was off in his own world, devouring the secrets of Shambala; he just loved it. 'But how can you read it if you know it's crap?' I wanted to know. 'I *knowingly* mix crap with reputable sources because reputable sources are invariably *boring* but there's a lot of *joy* in this crap,' he said to me back then.

'Listen, Josef...' I said.

'What?'

'You're not in the least mystified by what we saw up there last night?'

'No.'

'All right then... and what is a *succubus*?'

'Incubus and succubus, demons that appeared in order to shag people, in the dark Middle Ages,' he continued.

And I could see beyond any doubt that in his life he needed to see things from a distance, from safety. He was not afraid physically; once he let himself get two teeth knocked out, because of me, and he didn't bat an eyelid. But mysteries attracted him only as long as he had an 'access code'.

'And even in the eighteenth century they still believed, if you can imagine...' he was lecturing, fully engrossed, and I knew there was nothing else he wanted to talk about... 'And they didn't have to come in the guise of a human either, they could take on the likeness of a cat, billy goat, monkey, spider, anything; succubus is from the Latin 'succubare': to lie under, and in–'

'Enough, for fuck's sake!' I yelled and it sounded odd in the small space. 'Can't you talk to me for once about what we've *experienced*! What's this yakking for! You've witnessed something that you've never seen before in your whole life, and you yammer on about succubus!'

'So what do you want to hear?'

'Why you left me there alone with it!'

'What can I tell you about that! They were just animals, why don't you drop it... regular goats...'

'Bullshit!'

'We were exhausted.'

'Bullshit, you're avoiding the subject!'

'Take it easy, damn it, so what if we *may* have seen something we know nothing about, a couple of faces, all right, *ghosts*, some clowns that were no trouble, what do you want me to say?'

'So you *did* see it?' Now I really got pissed off.

'Yeah.'

'You *saw* it and left me there with it and fell asleep!'

'Yeah.'

'And what it was! Who it was! Doesn't that interest you?'

'No,' he repeated.

'And how do you expect to continue living with me?'

'Exactly the same way I have until now,' he answered in a strangely calm voice. 'We're fucked, Eva, all of us, whether we know it or not! You think you're something special?'

'Doesn't everybody think that about themselves?' I submitted.

'I think it stops working for you as soon as you start counting on it.'

'Well I think it actually works only as long as you expect it to...'

'I prefer counting on being a fucker.'

'How'd you mean?'

'Soft solution, I try being permeable. Many things pass through without hurting.'

I glanced at the cross sticking out of the gaping mouth of a dead body and instantly felt sick to my stomach. In that moment Josef approached and hugged me. I buried my nose into his sweaty shirt and started to cry like a baby. I cried and cried. I could still feel the callously indifferent stare of the man in the military hat earlier. I knew Josef was thinking about it too. Maybes and what ifs. He squeezed me against himself and rubbed my hair. I tried calming down, but to no avail.

'Some life, this is,' I sobbed. 'You don't even want to get me pregnant! We've been together for five years and nothing to show for it...'

'I'll work on it,' he comforted me.

*You're a cunt* – a faint tearful hurricane was throbbing inside of me – *Nothing but a cunt. It's all you'll ever be! Hysterical. Unfair. A cunt.*

'Really?' I muttered.

'Yeah. Now wipe your nose.'

I wiped my nose and looked at Josef.

'You're thin,' he said. 'When we get ourselves back down, we've got to grab a serious bite.'

I nodded. I was dismayed at how little I was feeling. The only thing I perceived was a quickly approaching shadow of a doubt which I'll perhaps never be rid of. It floated above me like a rain-soaked storm cloud. And it concerned not only me and Josef. It concerned absolutely everything. He was not a fucker. He was standing beside me, under that grimy cloud, as helpless as I was. The world was ruled by powers one could do nothing about. Powers one applauds until meeting them face-to-face. And when that happens, they blow you away in an instant, like a piece of paper.

'Let's get out of here!' I pleaded.

*Bang*, we heard. We both started. It was just a plank that had tumbled down from where it leant against the wall. The narrow strip of light revealed a fog of centuries-old dust rising.

# That Amsterdam of Yours is Somewhere That Way

We got out and had to avert our eyes from the welding flame of the solar disk for a long time. Large, awkward, brick-red letters carved across the front of the church spelled: IRON MAIDEN.

We reached the place where the path definitely swerved downwards. It meandered in and out of sight like a dried up earth-worm stuck to the pavement, and led to the flatlands. The wind was blowing against us, and we could easily lean into it.

'We got at least half a day's hike ahead of us,' commented Josef. He was shielding his eyes, gesturing with his hands, and then opened up a map, which I didn't even know we had, and studied it for a long time. The map rustled and flapped in the wind, breaking apart; Josef would stubbornly straighten it, and the wind would always rip it apart.

'South, north, northeast, this is where we are... So that Amsterdam of yours is somewhere that way.' He pointed towards a pile of clouds on the horizon.

'We should've gone there instead,' I said quietly.

'Next time we will.'

Pastures and meadows spread out below us. There was a legion of tiny houses with sagging red roofs, little sheds, hen-houses, enclosures, small open spaces, trees with broken off branches, decrepit walls. All that jumbled-up mess, riddled with corridors, bored through and parceled-up, decorated with faded postcards, shoelaces and papers and stickers and dolls. The mess we couldn't wait to return to.

'So did your father travel around with you like that, your whole childhood?' enquired Josef.

'My whole childhood until I was six... Except for his holidays.'

'How so?'

'For his holidays he'd go visit Čačko in the Novohradské Mountains.'

'Who was Čačko?'

'He was half Gypsy. They knew each other from their military service, and they'd go hunting ducks together. Čačko had this stick with a rifle hidden inside.'

'A gun, eh?'

'A shotgun, yeah, a regular walking stick with a shotgun inside. He called it "going quack."'

'Going what?'

'Quack, you know, duck hunting. I only met him about three times, but dad would go visit him every fall for two whole weeks. Apparently they had a special way of roasting those ducks, making them really delicious.'

'I see... so do you know how they roasted them?'

'No. I just know they were really delicious.'

'Mm,' Josef grumbled, unsatisfied.

'And Čačko also ate hedgehogs,' I recalled, a hundred metres further down. 'Once dad brought them home in a jar, already made. He just warmed them up and served them to my mother and me. And of course he only made the announcement when the pot was empty, and was about to have a good laugh at his clever little prank, except Mum simply wipes her mouth and says: "That was absolutely divine! My mouth is still watering. Next time you should bring more of those!" And only after having her coffee did she secretly sneak out to throw up...'

'So how come your father, a professor, was friends with a poacher from the mountains?'

'Maybe because he was able to live in his own way, which Dad could never do – he just thought and dreamed about it all his life. But Čačko actually lived that way – shot a duck, cooked it, ate it, met a woman, seduced her, then left... It's true I can't imagine what the two of them could have talked about for two entire weeks; maybe they were silent...'

'Did he have any kids?' Josef asked sternly, because he'd obviously been pondering the subject for a good hour.

Considering whether, after all, it may not be prudent to leave me while there was still time. Because my biological clock was ticking. But what would he do without me, right? Besides, we loved each other and couldn't live without one another anymore. But then again, what about the nightmare of having a little brat? He knew I knew he was thinking about it.

'Probably,' I said. 'With all the women Dad believed he'd had and envied him for.'

'Hm. How did he prepare the hedgehogs?'

'Roasted and pickled, grilled herring-style – bone-in, that is...'

'Yak, yak!' Josef shouted exuberantly.

'Oh, but it was good!' I said. And I was thankful for a past that I could always resort to. And I didn't have to reveal that I was the first to throw-up back then, always finicky about meat, having only schnitzels or breasts, maybe Hungarian salami, basically a spoiled brat: 'I don't want a rissole!' I would whine, and Granny, with her saintly patience, would take it away and go and make something sweet for me instead and then walk around the backyard picking wild strawberries from the grass by the fence, puffing and straightening herself up, pushing her hair – which she dyed blonde all her life – out of her face before coming to me with a handful of strawberries and I just went 'yum-yum' and gulped them all down...

Suddenly I was flooded with memories. In high school I still wouldn't eat rissole; when the class went to help with potato harvest it made me the butt of everybody's jokes, except for this one guy whose last name was Beroušek. He and I went as far as him showing me the spontaneous rippling of the skin on his balls, with all the intricately animate waves surging, swaying and rapidly flowing back and forth, which at that age was a stunning revelation to me. I was so captivated by it that I lost interest in progressing any further and became immersed in the detailed observation of

Beroušek's testes for so long that he got offended and left.

There were butterflies fluttering among bushes covered with tiny prickly foliage.

'And something else I remember...' I continued. 'This Čačko man once joined us on a walk. Dad was holding me by the hand as we walked to the lake for a swim, and Čačko caught a butterfly in flight just like that, some poor little moth, and he formed a little cave of sorts with his hands so I could have a peek, he held it before my eyes and said: "Take a look Eva, this is Mr. Death's Head von Hawk Moth, the next highest rank after the Red Admiral. He's in command of all the caterpillars and dung beetles around!" And then he let him go... That's how he was, fun and strange.'

The village was fast approaching. Jagged white cliffs that looked like a pile of broken mugs were flashing a toothy grin below us. We still had to hike through those to get to the flatland. There were droning whirlwinds gusting past us. One minute, the wind would swell against us, cooling our sweaty garb, and the next minute the roaring would stop and we'd find ourselves in a place of complete calm.

A lonely sheep was standing on a steep little meadow by the path, smiling at us.

'That's exactly the expression on my mother's face,' whispered Josef.

The sheep kept turning its head towards us until we were out of its sight.

We walked on and on. At one point we got pinned to a boulder beside the path we were on by an unexpected gust of wind. We sat down at the leeward side, took our shoes off and rested for a while.

'You know that in your favourite Amsterdam...' said Josef, lighting a cigarette, sucking his cheeks in, then exhaling a strip of smoke, 'in your Amsterdam in the eighteenth century, one of the most popular forms of entertainment was visiting a madhouse, paying an entrance fee and in doing so obtaining the right to poke at the caged lunatics with a stick and watch them rage. For an extra fee chairs were brought in and the whole family could split their sides at the loonies going berserk...'

'That's so mean,' I said.

'It is.'

'What else?'

'What else, they also went to prisons where for a pittance they watched people awaiting execution. They'd offer them roast meat and find it hilarious that those poor souls who had been eating nothing but rotten turnips all their lives now don't even have an appetite for duck thigh...'

'I would still like to see that place one day,' I said.

'Sure, if you want to.'

Leaning on the rock reminded me of another story, but this one I kept to myself. It happened during that same walk, we were walking on a meadow towards a forest, my hand in Dad's, when we suddenly heard this unsteady rattling and whirring coming from the forest, as if someone was riding a little wooden bicycle there.

'A nightjar,' said Dad. But Čačko's eyes instantly turned frightened and carp-like grey and there was a black wart on his temple with drops of sweat around it.

'Hey, don't be saying that to her.' He spoke quietly. 'What nightjar? That's not a nightjar...'

'So what would it be?' asked father. Čačko leaned over and whispered something to him. Dad looked at him in disbelief. And I got really terrified. I was on a walk with two adults – one was scared by something, and his fright got the second one frightened as well. 'Come on, you don't believe such stuff,' objected Dad, but Čačko just sped up, certain in his conviction.

The wind behind our backs howled again. The sleeve of a jacket flapped in the wind.

'This is a real howler we're in the middle of,' Josef said, changing the subject.

'That's a *howlie* or *howloon,* as in typhoon.'

'You and your imagination,' he responded.

When we put our shoes back on and got up, the wind was gone without a trace.


We walked on and on. The village was by now close enough for us to see the flowers in the window boxes. A dray drawn by a pair of horses was rolling down the road. In front of a fence at the edge of the village sat a burned out armoured carrier in the middle of a circle of blackened ground. Houses were dozing off on the other side of the fence. In their midst was a village square with a pointed bell tower. Our car was parked somewhere beside it. If it was still there, that was. Ding-a-ling went the bell. And shortly after a rooster crowed.

# The Evening

*Evening at last*
*every man for himself*
*matrices squeak*
*a hunting horn echoes*[22]
Ivan Wernisch

THEY LAY IN bed beside each other, staring at a painting. There was a line of poplars in the painting, meadows spreading far and wide, and seriously curly storm clouds.

A woman's laughter could be heard through the wall. Then it changed into a regular moaning.

'Stupid cow,' he cursed.

'Who is?'

'The woman next door.'

'You write everyone off in no time...'

'She is a stupid cow.'

'She's cheery, that's all... She sees men...'

'She can have all the men she wants, that don't bother me!'

'So what does bother you?'

'That she listens to Drupi ad nauseum!'

'Why shouldn't she listen to Drupi?'[23]

'Because Drupi is what hookers in Karlín listened to twenty years ago!'

They lay in bed looking at the painting. The roof of a farmhouse peeked out from behind a hill. The frame was a bit cracked. It had been hanging there for four years already. That's what they saw every time they fell asleep and every

22. Last line originally in German.
23. Male Italian pop singer who rose to fame in the 1970s.

time they woke up. And especially every time they lay there like this, rehashing something.

'So why don't you try seeing a psychologist about it...' she spoke softly.

'Psychologists, c'mon, what do they know? Psychologists are snobs who have no time for or interest in finding out how things really work in life,' he fumed. 'Besides, it's not exactly free. A psychologist will rip you off before you know it.'

'So why not try a...'

'A psychiatrist? Am I nuts or what?'

'Not a psychiatrist, a sexologist.'

'Those are even worse!'

'So what the heck do you expect me to do, I'm at my wits' end! We haven't slept together in a year and a half: how do you think I should cope with that!'

'Stop yelling!'

'That's all I ever get from you, *stop yelling!* Why don't you at least try seeing someone about it?'

'Because I already know myself what there is to know about it... There's nothing wrong with me!'

'Except you haven't been able to get it up for two years now!'

'That's not the problem...'

'Yeah, I know that's not the problem because you have a hard-on every morning, but when we're about to make love...'

'Jesus Christ, drop that self-help lingo, *make love...* I guess we just can't be spontaneous anymore.'

'*I* can be spontaneous! So what is the problem? Tell me, do you find me *repulsive?*'

They were staring at the painting. The sound of phoney suffering in the voice of the Italian singer came through the wall.

'How could you even think something like that!' he said. 'I love you, I've never loved any other woman the way I love you. I don't know what the problem is, something inside is missing for me.'

'So why don't you see someone about it like I've been

telling you all along!'

'It's not something for a doctor, they're clueless and have the same problem as everyone else.'

'What do you mean?'

'It's hard to talk about it.'

'Why don't you give it a try, you've practically stopped talking to me altogether! How am I supposed to know what's going on inside you?'

'Nothing – that's the problem – so how can I tell you?'

'What do you mean, nothing?'

'There's nothing happening inside me! That's the best description I can give you... That's all I can tell you!'

He seated himself in the adjacent room and just sat there for a while. He turned the computer on.

The taskbar announced – *Number of new messages: 1.*

The message read: *Welcome to the Death Clock™, the Internet's friendly reminder that life is slipping away second by second. To view your Death Clock, simply enter your birth date and sex in the form below and hit the button.*

Although he was not a big fan of this type of amusement and typically would delete it right away, he couldn't help chuckling at this one. He filled out the columns. Day of Birth: 21; Month of Birth: March; Year of Birth: 1963; Sex: Male; Mode: Pessimistic. He clicked and read: Your Personal Day of Death is Sunday, October 20, 2013.

He glanced at the clock. Quarter to three. He clicked the icon in the lower left-hand corner and then clicked *load game.* Suddenly he found himself in a wide, dark corridor with walls consisting of rusty metal slabs with coarse rivets.

A wart-covered hulk popped out from behind a pillar decorated with the patterns of screaming skewed faces, swiped his talon, chattered the white teeth in his hideous apish snout and exclaimed: 'Ue, ue!' A gunshot rang out and the monster got flattened against the wall, green shit splattering everywhere. The gun jerked, the left hand pulled the forend, tossed the cartridge out and reloaded.

# The News and Views

1.

AT AROUND TEN I swung by the bank to see if by any chance any money had come in.

'Ya got twoooo thousin' five hundrid,' said the clerk.

'That's too bad.' I feigned disappointment. 'OK, I'll take the two thousand.' I took the money and went directly to the butcher's shop. There were three female assistants standing behind the counter. I was looking at the iridescent bright red tendons, lined up regiments of pink cutlets, white sheets of bacon, capriciously rolled up red gristles, klobásas, salamis, and rough beef tongues smoked to a copper colour. Hanging from hooks were pork knuckles, hunks of smoked meat and ribs like blinds in a window.

A smooth male voice on the radio recited the news: 'A human arm wrapped in plastic was found in a garbage container in the District of Prague 6, and according to the initial police report belonged either to a young woman or a juvenile...'

'*Grosssss!*' shouted all three assistants spontaneously.

'...the police therefore ask residents who may have noticed anything suspicious during the specified period,' the velvety voice smoothly continued, 'to immediately contact...'

'May I help you?' asked the youngest.

'This turkey breast over here, about a kilo please,' I pointed.

The girl tossed the meat on the scale and twittered, 'Is two kilos too much?'

'That's too much. Could you cut some off?' I said.

'How's this?'

I nodded.

The butcher swiped the chunk of meat, from which she easily separated the tip, slapped it on the scale, and I gave her the money.

Back home I cut the meat thinly, added salt, pepper, thyme and rosemary, placed the slices in a pan with hot oil and put potatoes and broccoli on to boil next to it. The kitchen sizzled and steamed and the world behind the window got to be one shade brighter.

'Damn, that sure smells good!' came a voice from the corridor.

2.

At around three thirty it started to snow lightly. I found myself standing with a full stomach at Charles Square beside the Eliška Krásnohorská statue, waiting to go for a bit of a walk with Mikeš. After a while I started pacing to warm up a little. Eliška's eyes were like boiled eggs; she bore ever-more resemblance to a newt in formaldehyde.

'Would you happen to have a cigarette?' someone uttered into my ear.

A woman in her mid-twenties was standing there.

'Last two, I'm sorry.'

'Aren't you gonna buy some more?'

'I'm in my thrifty period, you know.'

'I do,' she nodded. She had astonishingly honest, pure eyes. And a strange, sped-up diction. She spoke as if at the beginning of each sentence she was throwing herself into the darkness among monsters. As if she was working her way through a dark forest. And her curly hair splashed about her round face.

It made me reach into my pocket, 'All right, I got six of 'em here, help yourself.'

She had me light it up for her.

'Beautiful snow,' she pointed to the sky with her cigarette.

'You bet, I'm glad.'

'Me, too, but it's cold. Got a little date here?'

'I'm meeting a buddy.'

The woman nodded. She was wearing knitted leggings. A skirt. A little jacket. A scarf around her neck. I was thinking what else I could say. A freshly completed glass box was towering above the crossroads.

'I don't mind when they put up new buildings,' I said.

'Me neither,' she said.

'I didn't even mind when they blew up the old Tatra factory in Smíchov and built Carrefour there instead. But that,' I pointed to the building, 'that is too much!'

'Think so?' She re-examined the cube. 'Yeah, it's horrible.'

'Super-horrible,' I added.

'It's freezing cold,' she shivered. 'When it's this cold it's best to climb under a duvet, huh?'

'I don't think so.'

'And a bit of sex too...'

'Oh, forget about sex,' I droned and blew my nose for no particular reason.

'So what else in this weather?'

'Well, like I said, a walk with a buddy, a couple of beers and home.'

'As you wish... But I would do it to you good, for four hundred. Or three – you're pretty nice.'

'No really, thanks.'

The woman shuffled her foot and tapped the ash off her cigarette. It was obvious that she hadn't slept around that much, but for some reason she really needed the money. Her irises looked as if they were composed of two transparent light-brown layers. One could travel in them. I was switching from background to foreground and felt like that celluloid ship that goes back and forth in a promotional pen.

'So two hundred then?' she said.

'No really, I'd rather just chat with you over coffee but

there's no time.'

A text message vibrated in my pocket: *Sorry, sick, in bed, wolfing down some ham from Pavlína, and watching Crime Site Munich. Let's do walk another time. M.*

Where are we, I thought to myself. Where are we and what the hell are we doing here? Whatever happened to goofing around? Lately we've just been rattling our mouths over and over, bitching about the same things and laughing at the same things. Where's the humour? What happened to those times we drank all night and listened to a load of rock and roll and then went to work in the morning? Now we just go for walks and rattle our traps, and even that's no fun anymore!

'The little date's not happening, eh?' she remarked jovially.

'No, my buddy's watching TV.'

'I'd also like to watch TV.'

'How about a coffee then?' I asked her.

'Really?' she said suggestively, 'or how about going over to your buddy's to watch TV?'

'He lives far away.'

He didn't, but like I said.

'I knooow already,' she whined. 'So let's meet in the café over there, all right? I'll just take care of some business here and then catch up with you.' Her teeth chattered and she disappeared into an underpass. A minute later she was happily showing me a little plastic package hidden in her hand. 'Don't you want some, too? I could go get you some, but you'd have to put up some cash for it.'

'No, no,' I waved my arm and felt a noticeable cranial kind of desire just like the urge to scratch oneself where a scab used to be. 'I gave that up a long time ago.'

3.

'I got it under control, this,' she assured me after we sat down, 'I don't even inject it, you knooow...'

I nodded.

'Yep, a little line now and then and that's that,' she said and averted her eyes.

'Hm.'

'You're not using anything?' she asked.

'Why?'

'Just 'cause, everyone's using something...'

'I just have some mushrooms once in a while and that's enough for me.'

'So what's it like, mushrooms, is it a sort of an *upper*?' she inquired.

'Not exactly, it's sort of pretty clean...'

'Like what do you mean?'

'Compared to this crap it's much more peaceful.'

'And you get smashed on this *every day*?'

'Oh no, not at all. Once in three months me and a couple of buddies drive into the woods, away from people, eat it there, lie on the moss until the evening, then sleep over in a sleeping bag. In the morning we pick up our shit and get going... The last time was in September, when we dragged ourselves up Milá Mountain in the Stredohorí Highlands where it's so beautiful as it is, we felt bad to be using anything in addition: hundred year-old ivy-covered trees, stones overgrown with moss, and up there on the peak a green carpet of wormwood, just like a little Japanese garden... So we ate it and waited. And this one buddy – he used to be a dentist – all of a sudden grew restless and kept saying, "I don't feel a thing, do you? I don't! It's weak! It's not working! Do you feel anything?" And I was afraid that he was gonna spoil it with his restlessness, that it wasn't gonna work the way it should because of his chatter, so it occurred to me to distract him. "Vítek, since you used to be a dentist, would you mind having a look at my gums, I think I got some sort of inflammation there, what do you think, should I have it checked?"'

'Did he quit dentistry 'cause he was tired of looking people in their gobs?' she asked.

'He quit because his colleagues in the field made him sick because they're apparently a bunch of mafia hogs. He insists he has known a lot of those who drill perfectly healthy teeth just so that they could milk some more money out of people... And so Vítek looked in my mouth and said, "What the hell is this here? I've never seen anything like that before! How long have you had it?" "A few months," I said. "Man oh man! This is the first time I've seen something like this! If I were you, I'd have it checked right away..." So I was panicked, of course, the first thing I thought of was *cancer*!'

'Haw, haw,' she giggled.

'I was about to close my mouth, but he shouted, "Hang on, hang on, hold it up this way, I gotta have a look at this, this is *interesting*!" and the other buddy joined him and both of them were staring into my mouth on top of this Milá Mountain, bug-eyed, saying, "This is strange! What could it be, my oh my? So purple! Orange! So in-teres-ting! I haven't seen anything like this my whole life!" And I stood there, perhaps ten minutes, looking in the sun, holding my lip and showing them my gums until I realized that this was not about my trap! Their gawking had finally got things started and my trap opened some sort of tunnel into another world for them...'

The woman stared at me wide-eyed.

'Really?' she said in amazement.

'Hang on, just a sec, I'm telling you this for fun, it's really just a banal story...'

'I understaaand,' she said and kept looking at me as if I had two heads. 'So what happened then, tell me!'

'Well, then all three of us finally got it going, so we lay in the grass and observed how the humming of the whole countryside gradually made its way to us. And then I suddenly heard this sound, as if a helicopter had turned its engine on next to my head, *vshu vshu vshu vshu*, so I jumped up and looked to see what was happening. And it was a brimstone butterfly that flew by...'

'Huh!' shouted the woman and grabbed the table, almost toppling it over and looking just great.

'What's going on?' I asked.

'Nothing, it's just that you still haven't told me what it's like, on mushrooms.'

'Quick or slow – it depends on where you are. In any case, you experience everything pulsating: everything's just waves on different frequencies, words, space, colours, it all falls apart and then comes back together like Lego. You experience all the ticking and rattle that you consist of. There's no matter, just a silent agreement among the molecules... You simply take a peek behind the curtain and it makes no difference from which side; you can have a blast and it can be deadly, but you can't take any of that back with you. Everything stays there...'

'I know.'

'I bet you do.'

'Know what, I'm gonna just sort of step out a bit and maybe have another java with milk,' she said, and walked away towards the back somewhere wiggling her arse, not that she wanted to, but she just was that way.

A minute later she danced in wearing those leggings like mama's little treasure at a school open house. Her nose spattered with freckles. Pupils like two plates.

'So where are you frommm anyways?' she asked when she sat down.

'Me? From here, Prague, and you?'

'Probably from a different planet, some place really far away,' she said and smiled. And behind that smile I caught a glimpse of the kind of weariness not known by those who slave from nine to five and fill the air with talk and buzzing and have their radios on loud at the same time, and then go home for dinner, because they are the main reason for that weariness.

'But I have no place to live here, which is sort of pretty bad,' she added absentmindedly.

'So, where do you sleep in this weather?'

'I've just said that I have no place to live, right... But I do have like a place in Prípotocní Street, a little plaaace... The trouble is that I can't stand being alone, you know? There's always someone staying over. The last time, I lived with a guitar player, a young wanker in leather. I don't know what I saw in him at all. He was as good looking as a skinned orangutan, but sometimes he was nice to me – you don't need much, right? The heart is stupid...'

'Yeah. And where did he play?' I asked.

'That's the thing, he didn't play anywhere because he was a troublemaker, and when he drank he acted-up. Other than that he was cool. It's just that he always wanted to sort of change me. When I'd tell him something he looked at me like... what's the word?'

'Vile? Vicious?'

'*Vile* is nonsense and I didn't mean *vicious*. He looked at me *hatefully* like what I was saying was idiotic and boring. And when I was silent, he smashed things and blamed me saying this was no life, not talking to each other, that it pissed him off when not even that tap would speak to him. So I asked him, 'So what do you wanna talk about? Tell me and we'll talk!'

And he shouted, 'Don't know! How the fuck should I know! I don't know!'

'It's like that everywhere, people live beside each other and they're afraid to keep going and they're even more afraid to end it,' I said.

'I know, but this started to get really sort of shitty. He started to stare at me strangely, didn't speak, listened to the

Ramštjans cranked all the way up and was as pleasant as water in the stomach, you know. I knew him, so I knew he was nuts and that he was positively gonna do something. And do something he did. Once he got up at night, I was sleeping like a pimpernel...'

'Like a pimpernel?'

'Yeah, sleeping like a pimpernel, he must've put some shit in my drink, some fucking sleeping pill, because I didn't wake up when he was tattooing me...'

'Tattooing?'

'Yeah, he tattooed me all over, he had a tattoo gun.'

'Really?'

'Yeah, he wrote all over me and took off. Look.' She rolled up her sleeve and showed me a row of thin bluish letters, that spread unevenly across the top of her arm: THE LEFT ARM OF A SLUT.

'My legs, look.' She pulled up her skirt and rolled down her leggings. Good thing we were sitting in the corner. White thighs with fine dark hair on them appeared: THE RIGHT LEG OF A SLUT. THE LEFT LEG OF A SLUT.

'And look over here,' she pulled down her skirt and hiked up her sweater and t-shirt. I saw an alabaster stomach. Her navel looked out at me from under its smooth, somewhat swollen eyelids. I LOVE YOU! was written right above the navel in an arc as if it had an eyebrow. FUCK ME! I'LL GO TO HELL! was written on the opposite side below the navel, also in an arc, but upside down. And below that was something of a line downwards.

'Watcha got there?'

'This is sort of an arrow,' she said.

I felt a sweet longing in the nether regions. Unwittingly I remembered the legend about a painter who was painting the Devil; the Devil showed himself to him in parts because if the painter had seen him completely, he would have been done for then and there.

'And look at this.' She showed me a tiny diamond

shape on the upper edge of the pelvis and then quickly hid it again. I noticed a comic speech bubble rising from the diamond shape and in it was a word, but I didn't have time to read it.

'I'LL HOLD IT UP FOR ANYONE, it says on my butt, but that's not true at all,' she whined. 'And the places you'd sort of ask about anyway he skipped over, otherwise I'd probably have woken up... Only here,' she pulled down the collar of her sweater and revealed the upper part of her defiantly shaped breast. There was a skinny saw-toothed little figure with a circle with two holes for a head, crosshatched trunk and four lines, arms, legs. Above the figure was written: FAREWELL! and below WE'RE ALL GONNA DIE ANYWAY.

'That's the only one I can agree with,' she commented matter-of-factly. 'When I get some money, I'll have the lines removed, but maybe this one I'll keep. Do you know where they do this kind of removal?'

'Dunno. Once I had a tattoo on my back, but a few weeks later it got inflamed and drained out by itself.'

'That's all I need right now.'

'Right. But what about that guitar player?'

'What about him, I haven't seen him since.'

The woman leaned her head against the back of her hand and suddenly a quick tear slid down her cheek.

'It's all falling apart for me,' she sighed. 'What am I doing here, such a simple question, and I don't even know that... What the hell am I doing here?'

'Nobody knows.'

'But I think to myself more and more that I'd be glad if those terrorist dudes just blew everything up here. The War of the Worlds – you know what I mean? Because anything's better than this day-to-day stuff.'

'I wouldn't be glad,' I said and listened to the sugar quietly pouring from side to side in the elongated sachet I took from the saucer. 'Because I think it would be more fair if it all fell apart by itself, without anybody's help, and it's falling apart already anyway.'

'I love coffee, I love tea…,' she hummed. 'But it won't be that way.'

'Why do you think so?'

'Because we're living only sort of in our thoughts, you know? We're so out of it that we're not strong enough to clear out the parade while we can... We're living only on words... Someone's got to help us!'

'I could only respond to that with words.'

'Well words, then. Go ahead and say them... All my pals who managed to get themselves out of this shit-hole suddenly started to sort of *believe*, and they got words for everything... Supposedly they learned something about themselves they didn't know, in one moment of truth, and therefore they will be *forgiven...*'

'What shit-hole?'

'Doesn't matter, this involves all of us, right, *forgiven*, what kind of bullshit is that? Forgiven by whooom? For two hundred thousand years we've been wading through shit, and keep hoping that someone's gonna forgive us... Who?'

I caressed her hand.

'And stop caressing me,' she said hastily, 'or no, caress me...'

I was rolling the sachet of sugar in my fingers; it felt like holding a fat and light caterpillar. I squished it and it burst. How could it be that an ordinary slut from Charles Square... Or isn't she a slut? How could it be that she can define it better than all those university graduates with two degrees?

I poured the sugar in my cup. A stray fly landed on the table and started to clean its front legs. The woman gently pushed it forward with her finger. The fly crawled forth a bit. She pushed it again. The fly crawled forth a bit again. '*Am I the last fly, bzz, bzz, my heart wants to cry,*' sang the woman.

A tall guy in his early thirties with a dyed matt black fringe carefully swept across his forehead came in the café, sat down and began to stare in the direction of our table. It's true he wasn't staring in a nosy fashion; it was like his mind wasn't there. As if he was still remembering fixing his motorbike that day.

The woman pulled up her leggings and smirked, 'Stop staring, stop staring, nincompoop!'

Dark Hair was staring and sipping his Becherovka liqueur.

'Kill the engine, you stupid moron!' the woman spoke quietly. 'Yeah, right! Dead beat!'

We chatted some more but the confidentiality of solitude was missing. The Dung Beetle kept sitting and interfering with our wavelength.

'Leave us alone and stop staring,' I said in his direction just for form. He didn't even look at me, just kept on studying the girl's small-town sweater.

'Are you insane. He could rrrrub you out,' she scolded.

'Maybe we can still go for a bit of a walk,' I tried to salvage the pleasant early evening chitchat. 'Or we can go grab a beer some place?'

'A little stroll, that would be nice. The last person who took me for a little stroll was my fatherrrr. I'd love to go... But you know what, why don't you tell me if you're interested or not.'

'In what?'

'You know... It would be sort of pretty pleasurable.'

I shook my head.

'So we'll do a little stroll some other time, OK?' she said.

I nodded.

The woman got up and stepped out again. On her way back along that hulk's table she bent over him and whined into his ear: 'Would you have a spare cigarette for me?'

The guy looked up, staring at her as if he'd noticed her

only now, and then nodded.

'Thanks,' she said and sat next to him.

The door slammed behind me and I was out. The snow was silently descending on parked cars. I looked inside through the glass. She was sitting there laughing. The dude was hunkered down, sucking his Becherovka liqueur and looked like a pumped up David Copperfield. The woman was shaking her curly head and chatting away. It looked like some horribly botched-up ending to a Christmas romance.

4.

I couldn't actually say, I thought to myself on the way, that I felt sorry for anything or anyone – myself included. But still, there's something to this way of being... Something in the way time treats material entrusted to it, or rather in the way we treat the time entrusted to us...

A man, the spitting image of the Neanderthal on a Zdenek Burián painting, stood on the tram island. He was holding a new stove pipe under his arm. It glittered in the approaching sunset as if it were alive. His white hair was blowing about over his low forehead. Beside him stood a woman with her hair cut short, compliantly watching the snowflakes disappear in a black puddle.

And women especially, I thought to myself, they take the weight of the world upon themselves at once, no talking back, many of them actually delighting in it, but none of them, excepting a few hysterical ones and exhibitionists, get all saintly about it! Women – all that's left to them is to live like saints! One saint after the other!

While contemplating I accidentally brushed against a pram going in the opposite direction.

'Watch it, you moron!' crowed the young mother.

'Kiss my arse, you stupid cow,' came out of my mouth to my own surprise.

For a moment the woman pointed her swarming crablike periscopes at me, then immediately forgot all about me.

A man on a motorcycle was charging towards me on the pavement. His rear view mirror flicked lightly, ever so lightly, against my sleeve and then was gone. I passed a few people resembling painstakingly made-up extras for a film set fifty years after a global nuclear catastrophe. A big fat blubbery lass, wolfing down a potato pancake in one bite. A horribly cross-eyed man with the leg of a horse. An old dolphin man with a smooth face free of any expression. A procession of tiny children with mean eyes and bat ears. A grandma with a small bald head and two or three wads of hair sticking out. She glanced at me, pouted her little goat-like mouth and cackled sharply.

A line-up of overcrowded trams was stuck in the street. Every five minutes one of them would furiously ring its bell, jerk and move two metres ahead. All the others repeated the move. Behind the sweaty glass the daily inferno was taking place; bunches of bug-eyed faces were gathered there, drops of sweat were condensing, stomach ulcers were bursting and gall bladders sploshing, there was silence and there was talking in Czech, Russian, English, the iron tongues of the North, the wooden ones of the Balkans and the watery ones of the East; there was shouting in German and whispering in Ukrainian and mumbling in Hittite, Chaldean and Aramaic. And there was in fact a feeling that all these languages were seamlessly melting together and into one another and that they were returning to their original state at a time when it was more than enough to grunt, boo, hiss, sputter, howl, and produce inarticulate roaring and all-encompassing laughter.

On the embankment, a tour of physically disabled people was moving forth. In the middle of the swarm of ostentatiously colourfully-clad bodies, strange hobbling, limping, hopping and shuffling was taking place. It looked like the city had been visited by some deep-sea-dwelling languidly-flapping creature, full of jerking decoys and lures.

Two girls with braids were standing by the railing,

watching swans. One swan was trying to take off from the water, but wasn't having any luck because it was dragging a long piece of wire wrapped around its leg. It was flapping its wings desperately and stretching its neck out. The girls started to laugh. Then a bunch of wantonly happy disabled people swarmed over them.

At the opposite bank a fireboat painted red was lightly rocking. It's been docked there at the pier for a couple of decades, and I've never heard of it taking off into any action. Actually it did once, I remember. It's true that, when the firefighters went on strike in ninety-one, they anchored their ship in front of the National Theatre and with great grandeur turned on the water canons, so that they could be called 'firemen' again The polished nozzles sprayed the silver and brown Vltava waters in powerful arcs to all sides while a crowd on the embankment watched on.

I rolled up my collar, crossed the bridge and headed down the spit-covered Lidická Street into the depths of Smíchov. Before the Andel crossroads I hung a right and carried on through the 14th of October Square. Using a crane, they were taking apart an old building. It resembled an ocean reef, there under a floodlight, behind the church. The arched alcoves and corridor entrances, with their patterned walls, were reeling in the sharp light, as if alive.

5.

I walked through the deserted Kartouzská Street. Tiny snowflakes descended from the sky, and behind all this glimmering and fluttering the gigantic wall of the Carrefour supermarket loomed, with an up-lit metal bridge stuck to the middle of it. I stopped for a while and looked. I felt like a tiny tourist who found himself at the foot of an overblown Egyptian tomb. And I couldn't help but see it: the fragile silver bridge even underscored a certain sick nobility of the building. Inhuman. But still noble.

A hill dusted over with white rose beyond the curve. Heck, I thought, that didn't used to be here, or did it? I stopped again and looked at an ordinary urban hill covered with bushes and trees. That's impossible, it must have been here, I thought to myself, full of uncertainty. But how come I never noticed it? Could I be coming down with something? Should I just go home and take some Ibuprofen? Or am I going nuts already?

I was so thrown off by the hill that I crossed the street, squeezed through a bush and started to climb the slope. I was walking on a path, looking under my feet and exhaling thin steam in front of me. Then I turned and took a shortcut on a steep grassy incline. The clouds ripped apart and a few stars glittered through the bare branches. *The further Genor ventured, the less lush the grass was; the hotter it was, the more noticeably the sun grew in size*, popped up in my brain out of context. *The sky was rising just a little faster than a slug* rattled in my head and squeaked like an old dictaphone, and into that I heard some urgent, ever increasing noise – but that was just ringing in my ear. *'You swine!' roared Genor, kicking her and neighing and bouncing, 'I'm a horse, I'm a horse!'*

Two tadpoles in hoodies were standing on the hill and making out below the trees. They paid no attention to me.

'Hi,' I said to them.

'Ciao,' hawked the lad. The girl sniffed uncertainly.

'I don't mean to bug you, I just need to ask about something...' I spoke in a somewhat muted way as if in a dream. 'It just seems to me that this hill didn't used to be here before. A strange question, I know but I'm not a psycho, I just... I just feel that this hill I'm standing on...'

'Well, it didn't,' squeaked the lad.

'It's been here only a year,' added the gal.

'A year and a half,' clarified the lad.

'Yep,' conceded the gal.

'I see, it's the dirt from the pit they dug up for Carrefour... But where did those trees come from?' I pointed to the fully-grown four-metre deciduous trees.

'Brought 'em in a truck, right,' explained the lad patiently.

'Rolled out the grass, stuck in the trees, right, and that's that,' rasped the miss. The lad sniffed uncertainly.

'That explains it then,' I said, again in a muted fashion. I left them to carry on making out, and came to the railing.

I was standing on a brand-new hill overlooking Smíchov. Lights glittered in the clear darkness, so clear as to give one a headache. It wasn't snowing anymore. The glass pit of Anděl gleamed like a melting iceberg. Something rustled under my shoe. A newspaper someone had tossed out. I wiped off the dusting of snow. HUMAN ARM FOUND IN DUSTBIN, PRAGUE 6 announced the headline. A supermarket shopping centre the size of a residential block silently lounged below. Fresh wind was breaking apart the clouds above the city.

I was standing on a hill in pitch darkness. And suddenly it occurred to me that actually everything was perfectly in order here. Absolutely everything. That those tin ideals, painted in screaming colours, which for millennia people had died for – good, evil, the truth, this and that – that they're still here, and yet fortunately no one takes them seriously anymore. Because every time these notions were publicly proffered, every time there was preaching about what's right and wrong, there was always someone with a bleeding nose and someone standing on a chair with a noose around their neck stiff from fear. It occurred to me that all it takes nowadays is to simply live honestly. And that there's no single reason to get upset over some insignificant details. That things have simply got as far as this and from here they will carry further. That it's not that we get what we deserve, but that things go through us and over us.

I was standing on a hill in pitch darkness between Kenvel and Carrefour; there was nowhere to step aside and no reason to step aside either. In paradise there was the rustling of paper and the sulking silence of the saints, while in hell the sweat of constantly screaming and screwing sinners sprayed all over; the stars were silent above and the roaring of lava resounded from below. I was standing on a heavy ship made of earth, full of cadavers engaged in lively conversation and squabbling, and the torn-up cob-webs of youth were flying from the mast.

And I was overwhelmed by an uncertain but unexpectedly strong feeling of happiness for living in exactly this time and no other, a time which is miraculous in that one can hear and experience and actually feel under one's feet this thundering blast, which is going to tear us away any time now, and descend with us again, ever lower, somewhere downward, into the unknown.

# Sightseeing Flights Over the Sea

We were sitting in a car, driving at walking pace on a battered road, me and an acquaintance. We were sitting in a car, our elbows sticking out of the open windows, idly chatting and following the unpredictable turns of the asphalt pavement above the grey, sluggishly rolling sea. We were staying at a guest house at the edge of a forest a hundred metres from the shore. Our wives were with us as well, but they would spend most of their time at the beach while we took slow, silent trips through the land of dwarfed pines.

One of those turns opened up the view of a field on which were perched three sun-blanched aeroplanes, two high-wing sports monoplanes and a corpulent, flaking biplane. A bent tin booth with a gigantic sign saying LOTY WIDOKOWE NAD MORZE[24] sat right by the road. A sun-tanned bulky man with a set of gold chains around his neck was loafing around on a seat inside the booth. He waved at us. My companion stopped the car, we got out and stretched our limbs.

'A gdzie można kupić takiego pięknego fordeczka?'[25] he asked straight away.

'In Prague,' revealed my acquaintance, as he was the owner of the vehicle.

'Praga, to znam, dobre piwko!'[26] the guy said, got up and brought three cans with the inscription *Żywiec*.

24. Polish: 'Sightseeing Flights Over the Sea'
25. 'And where can one buy such a lovely little Ford?'
26. 'I know Prague, good beer!'

'And where can you buy such nifty airplanes?' I asked.

'From a flying club. These are my planes! I'm retired so I make a living this way. I fly.'

The guy didn't look older than forty.

'You, retired?' said my companion.

'Yep. Retired. I'm a supersonic aircraft pilot, mister, fifteen years with the air force! Fifteen years of flying MiG 21s and look at me now! I fly old ladies in a old banger to see the ocean...' He pointed his finger at the airplane with the wide-apart wheels.

'That's a Wilga, right?' I noted.

'It's a Wilga, yeah,' confirmed the guy, 'and there's an AN-2 further back, but her engine's toast. I only fly the Wilga.'

A dusty dog was lying next to the booth, licking itself and lazily watching us. Warped, glaucous pieces of tin glistened from the nearby thistles. Something about them interested me. I went up to them and tried to see what they were. I saw some instruction signs in German and a set of front landing gear with a dual wheel. It was sticking out of the debris like the claw of a poisonous dragon.

'Hey, what's this?' I asked.

'That was a German F4 Phantom; it belonged to the Luftwaffe.'

'And how did it end up here?'

'I shot it down! Bang and down it went! Neah, just kidding,' he slapped us on the back. 'It fell in the ocean here last year during a navy exercise, and then our people fished it out... They were flying with it above the sea and it caught fire. And Germans? Boom – they bailed themselves out! A German, he'll survive anything. But we Poles do too!'

'We Czechs do as well, but differently from you and differently from Germans,' I said.

'Yeah, we know about that!' said the man. 'For instance, do you guys know why you didn't have partisans in Bohemia during the war?'

'No.'

'Because the Germans didn't give you permission! Ha ha ha, no offence gentlemen, just joking...'

I believe we had the odd one here and there as well, I thought to myself, but didn't say anything and went to inspect the remains of the Phantom up-close. The greenish, armoured windscreen was undoubtedly the most beautiful part. I knelt and observed the landscape through it. The German shepherd crept up to me and breathed on my neck. He licked my hand. Had a serious case of dog breath. Meanwhile, the guy and my companion were trying to outdo each other in their theories on how to beat life on its own turf. By this point they were already onto their third Żywiec.

I went around the kiosk to relieve myself. An old billy goat with bald patches stood in the shadow of the roof, plucking off thistles. And this billy-goat had a massive gold chain around his neck. A large gold cross dangled on the chain. I scratched the billy-goat on his bumpy scab-covered back and checked the cross. It bore a hallmark. The beastie was looking me in the eyes, while processing the dry weed with its hard lips.

'May I ask about the billy-goat back there?' I said to the man after coming back. 'What's the chain on his neck for?'

'It's because I can afford it, sir!' said the man defiantly. 'I've got enough money! I make a living!'

'I see,' I said.

'You don't believe me, mister?' asked the man.

'I do,' I said.

'If you don't believe me, mister, let me tell you something, do you see the dog?'

I nodded.

'So that dog's master was in Hamburg, you know Hamburg, mister? So that dog had a whore in Hamburg! The dog had a regular fuck with a whore! And do you know, mister, who paid for her?! I foot the bill for a whole hour!' The aviator slapped a barrel with his hand so hard it reverberated. 'A German woman fucked a dog! She wasn't into it but had no choice and you know why? Because money is money! Money is money, understand?'

'Sure, sure,' we agreed.

'Damn right! Another beer? C'mon guys, don't be shy... So what brings you up here anyway?'

'We're on a trip.'

'Here? But there's nothing around here!'

'That's why we like it,' we told him.

'What's to like about that? No chicks, no music playing, why don't you go dancing in the town!'

'Yeah, we will, we're heading for Gdansk in a few days.'

'Gdansk is a nice city... Gdansk was burned down after the war by the Russians, did you know that? Not Germans – the Russians did it! In order to spoil it for the competition! My Dad was in a concentration camp in Russia when he was forty, working. And he survived because there was a guard that looked out for him – why? – because he liked playing chess and Dad had been a Polish chess champ! So he'd always drag him out into a bunker and they'd play there while some poor devil next door, being beaten with a hose, was screaming. Bastards!' The man slapped a mosquito filled with blood against his neck. But there were camps way worse. This one provided labour for an arms factory, so they fed them okay there, if nothing else, even if some people disappeared from time to time, no one knowing where – whether they hauled 'em to Siberia or got 'em shot in the forest or even something worse, but that was the way it was... And after the end of the war my father was lucky to be able to come back. And this guard came to say goodbye to him and told him: "And why do you morons think you did so well during the war? What do you think you were fed? Where do you think we'd ever get meat for you! You were fed your comrades! You were fed Poles! We cooked soup from them for you, throughout the whole war!"'

We nodded again.

'And my dad was staring at him in amazement, not knowing if he should kill him then and there or thank him. So he did nothing and walked away...' The man finished his story, turned away from the wind and lit a cigarette with a large gold lighter.

We were returning through the silent countryside, weary from the sweltering heat. The winding road brought us into a valley. Our little guest house built from bricks with no stucco lay on the edge of a pine forest and resembled a sundried dead cow.

A note at the table inside our room read: *We're at the beach, see if you can find us! You're it... H. and R.*

The cold dusk wind blew in through an open window. A bird called out somewhere nearby. We locked the door, opened a bottle of Żubrówka and walked as slowly as we could on a sand path among sparse pine trees down to the beach.

# Stand Up for Yourself

*Disorder increases with time because we measure time
in the direction in which disorder increases.*

Stephen Hawking

'IT'S MY FOURTH today, but I'll have some,' said the thirty-something man with a reddish, somewhat pimply face and hair tied in a ponytail, who was sitting at my table. He shook his head and, taking the mug into his hands, glanced at the colour print of a chickadee on the porcelain, then took a sip.

I'd found him standing right in front of my door after I came back from my morning errands (newspaper, rolls and non-carbonated water from the Chinese shopkeeper across the street, who as one of my friends claims, is actually Kazakh). On my way back I noticed a green plastic chute hanging from the roof about a metre away from the building entrance, probably in preparation for another construction project, about the fifth in the last three years... The man was shuffling his feet in front of my door, studying the half scratched-off nameplate, and holding a leather briefcase behind his back.

'Can I help you?' I asked the standard question.

'Do you live here?'

'I do.'

'Then evidently you can help me. I'm a bailiff and I'm here by court order,' he said, and from his briefcase he pulled out a paper, thickly covered in writing with my family and first names all over it. National insurance. Including a penalty, it had accumulated into a sum which I initially found hard to believe.

I unlocked the door, offered him a seat and tried to lighten the situation: 'On the table before you is some fresh coffee which by all accounts no longer belongs to me. Would you like to drink it? There's no sugar in it.'

'It's my fourth today, but I will have some,' he said and took the mug in his hands. 'And I must say that I'm impressed by how well you're taking this. One doesn't see that very often...'

'What can I do, tackle you with an axe?' My voice trembled because I unwittingly thought of that stupid chute by the entrance door – the place will be a mess again, and then this on top of everything.

The man uneasily jerked his head and the muscles on his neck contracted. I took a brief look at him; the type of guy who becomes a teaching assistant after technical college, fathers a child on the side and is bright enough to realize on the other side of thirty that something somewhere hasn't gone quite right.

'I was joking,' I assured him. 'But I can see that you've been around.'

'It's not always easy. Recently a guy shot at me from a percussion gun, and he only owed fifteen hundred! People react differently. Some time back this young guy at Anny Letenské Street let me in, then climbed into bed, covered himself with the blanket, and from then on didn't utter a word – just watched me from his bed as I put warrant of execution stickers on all his furniture...'

'And probably some people don't even let you in, right?' I wondered.

'They don't, but in those cases I'm required to come back with a locksmith and a copper. The locksmith picks the lock and you get the bill, which can be rather costly, so I wouldn't recommend it... All right then. Let's get to it, what do you say?'

I followed him around and looked on as he stuck bright yellow tags stating SEIZED BY WARRANT OF

EXECUTION, DISTRICT COURT FOR PRAGUE 3
on my TV, stereo, computer and other such objects.

'Technically I could also seize your books, but I can see
that you love them, so I'll let it slide.' He tried to brighten
the mood. 'You like reading, don't you?'

'Depends.'

'I'm into books, too,' he said, 'big time.'

'Then he became interested in a four-foot tall wooden
carving of a wry-mouthed green troll. 'We could classify
that as a work of art,' he said. 'You mind if I put a sticker
on that too?'

'I'm certainly not giving you that one,' I resisted, which
got him interested. I told him the story of how a carver
presented me with it as a band-aid for my poorly-hidden
troubles with a girlfriend, and how we brought it wrapped
in a blanket all the way from Zbraslav on the first morning,
straight from a party. How we put it down on the ground of
the Smíchov Bus Station, shiny with grease and sticky with
soda, when it was still quite dark out. How an older Gypsy
man standing in front of a closed kiosk spotted us, summed
up the situation with his experienced, murky eye and how
he turned on the spot and hurried away because as far as he
was concerned the situation was clear: two stupid white guys
cut someone a little too hard and were now trying to get rid
of the torso of the body before dawn. And really, when we
took a look at our cargo, we saw a convincingly stiff greenish
face, plus right where we put the carving, there happened to
be an oily brown puddle.

The bailiff laughed and let me make another coffee for
him.

'It's already my fifth today. And which writers do you
like?' He returned to the books.

'Different ones, I always get really taken with someone
and I immerse myself in their stuff for so long that I know it
by heart and then comes a moment when I figure out their
formula and that's it.'

'It's no longer fun for you...'

'It's not that it's not fun, but the whole text somehow ceases to exist. It disappears. It's gone.'

'I know what you mean!' He rubbed his hands.

So we philosophised a bit. We tossed authors' names on the table like potatoes gone cold, poked at them with our fingers and tried quoting them. He liked Singer and Ota Pavel and äkvoreck˝, as he said, and of course Bukowski and someone named Robbins and also Meyrink and surprisingly Halas. And he dragged me to my own library and searched the volumes for his favourite passages, which were exactly those I disliked, and when I tried to pay him back in his own coin it was the other way around. With his eyes cast to the carpet he confessed to me that he also wrote a bit here and there. That he wrote poetry and really hated it when someone referred to poetry as 'rhyming'. And that lately he'd been trying to write short stories. I had to tell him that I could relate and that lately I had also been trying to write short stories.

'Look, l have a suggestion,' he put forth after a pause. 'Why don't we be on first-name terms, what do you say?' Just call me Honza, I know you're Honza too, it's in my paperwork,' he slapped his briefcase.

I shook his cold hand and offered a fifty-percent-alcohol pear brandy that had been kicking around my pantry for two years; not that it was bad, but it certainly wasn't good. I had a little snifter-full with him. The bailiff knocked back the shot, and I unwittingly perceived that somewhere here must be where the shoe pinches.

'So you could join us at Sázava,' he proposed. 'We have poetry get-togethers there so perhaps you could also do a reading... It's coming up in just three weeks.'

I uttered an unconvincing sound.

'By the way, what are you gonna do about your debt?' he switched back to the original subject matter. 'If you're broke, there are ways this can be taken care of, perhaps I could get you...'

'I can manage, in increments.'

'So why don't you make these payments right away?'

'Because my head is already cluttered with shit I'm forced to think about: bills, taxes, fees, late payments, this really is a direct assault on my time for one, and for another, why is the state, that solves everything either with tetracycline or by getting you under the knife, so concerned about my health?' I tried giving an honest answer and the young man frowned. 'Besides, I just forget to pay,' I added. 'It's laziness, I'm lazy as a pig,' I added, and the bailiff's face partially brightened up.

He held out his glass and I filled it up. He drank to me with a sweeping gesture and in the same moment noticed that a door in the kitchen had been walled up. I told him how, way back, a fire at my neighbour's workshop on the other side burned through there when he, apparently by accident, spilled some petrol on himself, and to complete the destruction, everything happened to catch fire – and how he'd haunted me for some time, so I decided to wall the door up. The bailiff rolled his eyes and, not asking for further details, poured himself another shot of pear brandy.

'I see lots of stuff myself.' He added his bit in a protracted tone of voice: 'I could write a *novel* about my work... But do pay your debt. I'm telling you Honza, they're such nasty sons of bitches you can't imagine. They'll seize your furniture, electronics, everything, give it away on commission while leaving you thinking that you can pay and get it back, but think again! By law they're required to publicize the date of the auction, but they arrange it so it's only put up on some out-of-the-way bulletin board at the end of a hall by the toilets, where no outside person ever sees it, and then they have their auction and buy it up among themselves at cut-rate prices and equip their cottage with it. And you've got no chance: you've paid off your debt and now you're sitting in an empty pad...'

I assured him that I would pay.

'Why don't you go to the district office, talk to this

person named Záluûná. She's on the second floor on the left. A chesty curvaceous lady, she's married to a police investigator and she loves riding jet-skis. Work out a payment schedule with her, she's easy to talk to...'

Finally he reminded me about the authors' reading one more time. It was supposed to take place in a church near T"nec nad Sázavou; it was organized by a bunch of literature enthusiasts led by this poetic bailiff. We said warm goodbyes to one another. This was on Monday.

On Thursday I set off for the office and on the second floor, in a room decorated with spiderwort plants, I found a pink blonde with a look in her eyes that was, at least on the verbal level, open to practically anything.

'Oh, Mr. Sinner,' she welcomed me after I introduced myself. 'My colleague Varvařovsk" has already told me about you...'

'Who?'

'Our junior, he mentioned you were joining him for their get-together to recite poems or something... Apparently you complained that your flat was haunted? That you can't get to sleep as a result?'

The employee at the other desk, with the face of a die-hard Prague Bohemians FC fan, looked as if he was trying to suppress a fit of epilepsy. I made arrangements for a payment schedule and got out. These are the levers – it dawned on me as I was descending the marble stairs – these are the gears running the engine of the state! It's not that a hundred rusty missiles get sold to Syria through Italy, it's that there are enough boneheads, who think that they can get away with not letting themselves get continually ripped off. The bureaucrats take it easy, wait a few years not to scare the little rebel, and once the penalty blossoms, ripens and grows, only then do they pounce.

The bailiff called me the next day to confirm I was really coming and he told me right out that Záluûná took to me, and if I wanted, he and I could take her out for a pint. He phoned a few more times in the following days. He always addressed me as 'Honza' or 'man'. The plastic chute assembled from segments remained suspended from the roof like the body of a cosmic worm, quietly dangling in the wind. One morning, with a rumbling and screeching, they put a huge metal skip underneath and covered half my window with it. An hour later I got a call from the bailiff, who wanted to make sure I didn't forget the event was taking place tomorrow and said they'd be expecting me and I should bring a sleeping bag.

*

The next morning I packed up and got onto a train headed for T″nec nad Sázavou, since it was easier than getting on the phone and making up a story about a sudden bout of a flu. I got off at Týnec and stood on the concrete platform for a while, peering at my zigzaggy little map. I had to walk back in the direction I came from, then along a creek towards some temporary buildings, from there to a chimney and from the chimney to a forest. The banana-shaped chimney on the piece of paper was producing an immense amount of smoke. So did the real one, which I was just passing. The forest was near. A sign on the first oak tree read:

## DOG OWNERS!

*Prevent your pets from running freely on the hunting grounds.*
*The wild animal population is being managed according to current legal regulations in order to preserve it for future generations. It is essential for wild animals to remain undisturbed in order to thrive, not only while laying eggs or rearing their young, but throughout the entire year. No living creature can be free without limits, for when it oversteps the bounds of its actual autonomy, it tramples upon other creatures. There are no known cases of dogs being chased by hares or deer; it is invariably the other way around as a result of the nature*

*of these animals. Only humans can moderate and guide a dog's behaviour in such a way as to ensure that the hunting grounds are utilized in a manner beneficial for hunting and game management as well as recreation. There is a further urgent reason for limiting the movement of dogs on the hunting grounds: bait is regularly placed in this area in order to vaccinate foxes against rabies. Ingestion may lead to health problems in your pet.*

*The Hunting and Game Management Association of*
*ZBOŘEN› KOSTELEC*

Stamped and signed. I read the text three times in a row with an increasing feeling of delight, and I noticed my soul for some reason becoming filled with peace. I felt a whiff of the deep pleasant smell of mycelium from the hollows underneath the moss. The sun quivered and hummed among the branches. I knew the autumn had begun again. Then I followed a signpost. The place was apparently called Ledce, and from the way it had been described contained no more than a church, a farm, a lake and a couple of houses. I already spotted a faded mound rising at the other end of the meadow, from which the house of the Lord jutted out like an endlessly repaired tooth from a jaw. Bitsy willows bristled compliantly from the field underneath. A gathering of people was milling about on the top of the hill. There were more of them than I'd expected, but it was too late to gracefully turn around and beat it since my mobile started to jingle in my pocket just then: 'Are you on the way? The meadow? Where... OK I can see you now, over there,' one of the figures was gesturing. 'C'mon, c'mon...'

Froth trickled from a small beer keg that had been tapped directly below the wall of the church, loaves of bread and meat loaf slices were lying about on a wet table, jovial highfliers with cup in hand shuffled around a well-trodden area, exuding the faint radiation of old gaffers that have been coming here with the gang for years, repeating whatever they had to say countless times. Their wives, with hairstyles that hinted at cherished memories of their high school rebellion, were humming nearby. Here and there a lone poetic creature would hover by, a few millimetres above the ground. Little brats were furiously riding their trikes and bikes around the building. Several young folks were waiting to see how all this was going to evolve.

The bailiff, fully occupied with organizing, gave me a slap on the back, called me 'Honza, my man,' and informed me that, as the guest, I would be the first to read in about ten minutes and I should get ready. There were chairs and a few planks laid on top of bricks, five or six mattresses placed on the rough stone floor and that was it. A handful of individuals were sitting in the cold air and quietly watching me. I read a short story to them. After I concluded, they clapped, and I thanked them and went out to get some fresh air. A short bulky fellow in a cotton army jacket with a collar turned up around his balding bulbous skull hurried out at the same time as me. There was something of the rhino about him. He walked towards me, stopped, and from a distance of four metres said: 'That's how it should be, you show up ssome place, ssay your bit and get out, right?'

'Oh yeah.'

'I don't mean to offend, ssaying thiss, becausse we don't know each other... I liked what you read, but not how you read it. You drag it out too much, but other than that it'ss great... To introduce mysself, I'm Sstanda Vanca, poet,' he said. 'Don't know if you're into thiss, but what you see here is Saint Bartolomej Church, originally romanessque, later rebuilt as baroque and now deconsecrated.'

'How does a church get deconsecrated?' I asked.

'The church lacks the financess, at least here in this region. I'm a heritage buildings conservationisst, sso I know. And I'm a bit of a Catholic too, if that'ss okay with you.'

I told him it was and we spent the evening in

conversation. We climbed the spiral stairwell up the bell tower and looked at the landscape through grey beams corroded by pigeon stools. Then we stood at the gallery in the shadow of the church organ, which was contorted and decayed as if from syphilis. 'Now we're at the gallery, which should always face easst, while the main tower facess west,' the poet whispered in a way that echoed. 'Sso when you get into a church, on your *left* iss your northern or episstolar sside ssince that's where the episstless are read and on *right* is the ssouthern or gosspel sside, where the gosspel is read...'

A smiling longhaired fairy was singing down below us. She was singing dolefully and playing a flute clearly and beautifully.

'Good girl, goody goody with clumssily shaved armpitss,' Vanča quipped from the gallery directly above the parting in her hair.

Afterwards we returned to the tower and watched everyone down below getting progressively drunker. The families were getting into their cars and driving away along the path.

'I love thiss moment, let me tell you,' declared the poet. 'When old friendss begin to pisss off and only the hard core remainss.'

When we came down for good, the bailiff was apologetic for not spending enough time with us as he'd been nervous about whether things would pan out okay. He said he'd brought his own short stories with him, and did I want to give them a read? He pulled a bunch of folded papers from his back pocket and passed them to me. He then went back inside, sat down, grabbed a guitar and without beating around the bush he struck a rough chord: 'Here comes a tractor, not detractor. It's a plougher, of mighty power...'


I haphazardly settled down for the night on the slope under the church, as there were no flat spots to speak of anyway –

the mound was sloped on all sides and at the bottom changed into thorny bushes. I lay on my back, zipped myself up and watched as the flickering fireflies silently scurried around the dark roots of the cosmos. Inside people were grinding their guitars.

I woke up in the middle of the night to discover that not only had I slid down into the bushes, but that during the descent, I had also exited my sleeping bag completely and was now lying with my face stuck to the ice-cold and tacky ground. After many attempts to at least partially bring my body back to life, I finally managed to get up. The mound was covered in darkness. Cold glimmers were flickering inside the church. I forced myself to take a few steps to check in the light of a flickering kerosene lamp that there was truly no more room among the tangle of bodies. I peered for a while at the heads hiding in sweaters, the feet stuck into backpacks in desperation.

I went down to the lake and walked briskly around it a few times. On my way back, I spotted a dark larva nestled in a inflated purple casing, which it was dragging behind itself, like the train of a wedding-dress, as it went around the building. A thick twisted horn was sticking out of its head. I stopped and waited for it to come closer. I recognized the Catholic poet Vanča stuffed into a myriad of shirts and jackets and wrapped head to toe in a sleeping bag.

'How now? Cold enough for ya?' he welcomed me after lifting the tip of his sleeping bag so he could see me.

'Fuck yeah.'

'B, v, v, v, v, v' he answered. 'Got a plan?'

'Pack up and go catch the train.'

'Would you be againsst me tagging along?'

★

The sun poked out its belly like a watchman from a prefabricated booth and shed its light on an ancient landscape licked by erosion. We walked along wetlands and weirs, on battered roads around the ruins of old breweries, and passed half-finished buildings under construction, which were themselves already starting to fall into ruin. Trees were wrapped in cobwebs with trembling fluffballs in them. And there was dew. And all that stuff. The trout warily moved their red fins at the bottom of creeks. Plastic sheets and macerated cement paper bags were floating on the surface.

'We can get to Poříčí on foot and take a bit of a walk, and at least we'll dry off,' suggested the poet.

'Good idea.'

'What do you do?'

'I'm an editing hack for a magazine.'

'Iss it good?'

'Not particularly.'

'So how do you know Honza Varvařovsk˝?'

'He was in charge of my warrant of execution.'

'Of mine too, that's how I got to know him.'

'Why does he do it?' I asked.

'Trying to make ssome dough,' answered the poet.

A heron took off from the bank, hastily flapped its wings just above the bulrushes, gained height, and began to soar.

'Way back in Hrochův Týnec when I wass a boy I sstole a matchbox car,' confessed the poet. 'It was an American jeep, but I lost it right away and only fourteen yearss later when I wass scything granny's grass, Honza, wouldn't you know it, man! I found the matchbox car lying there completely rusted! I'd already had a girlfriend for a long time by then, but when I saw that car, I could barely hold back the tears.'

We were wading through a flooded meadow. We had to take our shoes off because we were up to our ankles in water trying to find our way.

'And when I wass five, my uncle wass getting a nanny goat impregnated by a billy goat, and he told me to come and watch; my mother and aunt were trying to haul me away from there, right, but they were too late. And when they were bringing the billy goat in across the farmyard on a rope, even before sseeing the poor nanny goat, he wass already rehearssing and ssquirting in advance... It flew in a three metre radiuss ssplashing mom with jizz and everybody elsse. Such wass my uncle'ss humour...'

We walked through a landscape razed to a complete flatland; this was the work of yellow-painted bulldozers, graders and scrapers that crawled along the horizon, stripping away any remaining disparities.

'But I wassn't finished telling you, that girlfriend of mine knew I liked to indulge, sso to make me happy, sshe bought a backyard hen for me to roasst but didn't notice that the hen wass full of wormss,' the poet carried on. 'Sso I sscraped the wormss off and ate it sso I wouldn't hurt her feelingss, but I haven't chowed down on hen ever ssince.'

We were marching on a narrow path between two walls and thistles that were up to our shoulders.

'Actually I have, but I alwayss remember thiss... Got a girlfriend?' he inquired over his sshoulder.

'I do.'

'Iss sshe good in bed?'

'I think so,' I answered, caught by surprise.

'The main thing iss you gotta love her, women need that,' he nodded his round head while pulling the thistles apart. 'I got a girlfriend and I love her, but I definitely won't marry her.'

The path took us to the middle of the courtyard belonging to a farm building, where Gypsies were smashing apart old tables and chairs and loading them onto a flat-bed truck. When they saw us, they paused in their work and peered at us with eyes that were sunken like raisins in a bun.

'But truth be told, one doesn't need more than bread, salami, a little onion and eggs,' the poet continued undisturbed. 'No one says there's anything wrong with a bit of meat, but bread, onion and eggs are the nuts and bolts.'

We were passing through an orchard. A little bird was sitting on a fence, psychotically jerking its tiny head.

'A birdie,' Standa greeted it. 'I hear your place was haunted by a ghost or some such thing, Honza...'

I told him about my neighbour who'd died in a fire and about this stupid cow at a party I had a while later, who insisted on holding a spiritualist séance because she happened to be reading some sensationalist booklet about it, and of course nothing happened that day, but the following day, when I was there alone, I had a nightmare, and I saw myself lying covered by a duvet, unable to move, while from the place where the burned-through door used to be, the head of a fox was snapping at me, trying to bite my throat. And then when, with the greatest effort, I woke up and finally opened my eyes, I realized that I could really see something there nipping at my throat with all its might – it just didn't have the energy to touch me. Even so, I could feel such a high level of pure, concentrated hatred from that spot that I was pretty scared to sleep in that flat for quite a while.

'I see,' said Vanča. 'Sso you didn't actually ssee the ghost.'

'I did.'

'Sso what did it look like?'

'It had a chequered shirt on. I didn't see its face.'

'And it's gone now?'

'A woman came to live with me there who was in the habit of walking naked around the flat while performing breathing exercises, so maybe that helped. It's been quiet ever since.'

By this point we had reached a wide asphalt road surrounded by rusting, ancient linden trees. Standa gave a lecture about linden trees. About old, treed avenues. About the fact that a church spire is usually complemented by a smaller one across from it called a fléche, which sserves as a ssmaller bell tower sso they wouldn't alwayss have to bang about on the main bell.

'If you're ever in trouble,' he added casually, 'you can alwayss call on me. Like if someone wanted to beat you up or something, you're a friend and good guy so I'd help you out...'

We turned onto a footpath and walked through an open grove. Even though there was no wind, tiny, dry maple seed helicopters started falling from the branches at one point. The air around us was filled with these rushing woodland clowns.

'Like little noses,' I pointed out.

The Catholic poet swiped his short and stubby paw at them like a little bulldog trying to catch a fly, but caught none. 'Or if you needed a gun for insstance, one can get into a messsy situation,' he continued, 'I can get you a new nine, straight from the factory, sseven fifty six iss crap, with a nine you can just shoot the guy in the leg, and he goess down right away so you can bail out.'

'Maybe later on,' I said so it wouldn't appear I didn't appreciate the offer.

'You ever go camping?' he asked after a while.

'Used to, but not so much anymore.'

'What wass once will alwayss be, ssome time we could go on a trip.'

We were walking on a road towards a bridge under which the Sázava River snaked. A sign with the name of a town stood by the road. It was an ordinary sign but the name seemed impossible. I went over, to study the matter up close. I see, I see. It should have read POŘÍČÍ but the diagonal line of the letter 'Ř' had been painstakingly airbrushed out, as was its hook, making it into a full-blown 'P'[27]. The state of the sign on the other side of the road, indicating the end of the town, was no different.

'Jusst a little joke,' commented Standa.

27. Turning it into 'Cunt Town'

*

We walked among houses filled with the smell of burned stuffing before arriving at a small, deserted station with no departure schedule to be found. The bartender in a corner pub, which we discovered the very next moment behind a large pyramid of stacked up concrete railroad ties, silently pointed to the train schedule pinned to the wall, while getting us each a beer at the tap without uttering a single word.

At the head of the table, a fair-haired beanstalk with a moustache, sharp nose, overbite, and receding chin kept tossing his head to get a quiff of hair out of his eyes, which rather made him resemble a polecat: 'Been getting wasted for five days straight, man. You would too if you were expecting a baby! What a nail-biter! You can't imagine, dude! Major nail-biter!'

A shorter, yet still quite tall fellow, who looked like a copy of the taller guy, was slouched beside him, listening intently to his every word. About five others kept nodding absent-mindedly. Covering a portion of the wall directly behind them was a large fresco depicting a group of curious patriarchs holed-up around what was apparently the very same pub table the current ones were sitting at. A miniature waiter with a pencil behind his ear was walking towards them from the right, bringing pudding sausages. There was a bit of 'The Last Supper' in it and also a bit of an illustration attempting to convey the hallucinations of a Chinese opium smoker to a lay person. This was accompanied by the rhyme:

> *Lauřím's Pub in Poříčí*
> *Is certainly the place to be,*
> *At the lengthy corner table,*
> *Life is but a blissful fable*

*It is such a wondrous place,*
*Have a beer and stuff your face,*
*A game of cards or naughty jokes,*
*You'll have fun with our good folks!!!*

'So I was at the delivery, right, she'd wanted that!' the polecat said. 'I'd say every dude should experience that, man, cause it really is somethin' else! And I mean somethin' else!'

'That's fantastic,' a coarse doughy beauty intoned before finishing her beer, getting off her ass, and heading for the bar. Standa Vanca turned his hirsute head in her direction and it stayed that way. The beauty threw back her hair and with deliberation blinked her oriental-like eyes while ordering something.

'Shit, man!' continued the blond one. 'And then it started for real, right, the birth... And when it was poppin' out I realized I was still completely stoned... So it popped out, they dried it off, right... I picked it up with my hand, right, being the father and all. And I thought it was gross, d'you know what I mean!'

Vanca pulled away his chair, went over to the slit-eyed lady and without further ado started telling her something. For a while I watched her complete lack of surprise, simply listening to another voice. Then I returned to the faces of the patriarchs on the fresco. Everyone was there – the good man, the miser, the village know-it-all, and the one who's always all smiles, yet everybody's afraid of him. The dark hunter was there as well, a Bohemian Tartar in a fedora hat, quite possibly a biological ancestor of the round-assed chick into whose ear Standa was chattering something this very moment while resting his palm on the wet tin bar.

'Your own kid, man, you get it! I almost puked right there!' the blond man agonized at the table.

The longer I stared at the denizens silhouetted on the wall, the more I saw the familiar faces from the treasury of universal typology. One minute it was a brigade of overworked villagers, the next a gathering of dangerously jolly trolls. The actor Jiří Adamíra was having a drink with Ivánek from the Russian motion picture *Jack Frost,* while Joschka Fischer was looking over their shoulder.

'Holy shit, man, I'm a father!' the blond man hit the table so hard the glasses bounced. 'A father!'

I realized the poet hadn't been in the room for a while. I looked around and spotted him outside the window standing right next to her, yammering away. Slit-eyes was listening to him, her eyes closed in a state of bliss. I could see that she was hooked; that this crony, who was a head shorter than her, had managed in no time at all to get her onto his poorly greased verbal roller coaster, and that she was happy to go for the ride.

'What are you staring at!' the polecat with the quiff disrupted my observing. He was right, I was staring alternately at the wall and at them the way one stares into an aquarium in a waiting room, not actually seeing them.

'Just staring,' I said.

'Well quit staring! And chill out, buddy! And what's your fucking pal's business messing with our Majka!'

'I'm not his nanny.'

'So chill and go tell him to back off.'

'Go tell him yourself.'

'Easy, buddy! Chill back!'

'Hm,' I said. I had absolutely no interest in squabbling.

'Hmm what?! Hmm what?! Telling you to chill back!'

'I'll take care of it bro.' The one who resembled him got up.

'Don't be fucking with my bro – let's step outside, we'll take care of it!' his look-alike addressed me.

I went out and wondered what to do. Bro's bro rushed ahead of me and kept spitting tiny gobs on the ground. We stopped on a rutted grey area in front of the entrance. Bro kept spitting tiny gobs to the side. I figured it might be pertinent to let ourselves get pummelled a bit and get it over with. That this was maybe the simplest solution. He wasn't too steady on his feet anyway.

The poet Vanča emerged from behind the stacked railroad ties with slit-eyes under his arm.

'What the hell are you up to? You're sure not gonna fight!' he exclaimed as soon as he saw us. 'Just leave it for fuck'ss ssake! Issn't there enough mess already? Not enough guyss ended up locked-up as it is just cause some other guy fell the wrong way? Why not take a walk with us, eh?'

Polecat's bro kept silent for a while just for form. Then the four of us headed towards the power poles, whose arms stretched out above the shimmering hollows past the birch forest. The girl walked beside Standa; she was the kind raised by hippies, yet she exuded a sort of quiet acquiescence, which was why I understood why he was after her. The bro took out cigarillos and offered us some.

'I haven't ssmoked for three monthss,' Standa remarked matter-of-factly.

I helped myself to one.

'Look man, I'm a village guy, right,' the bro put forth. 'My bro's just had a baby girl, so we're celebrating. You got children, right?'

'Two,' I lied.

'So you know what it's about, right?'

We walked along a tiny creek until we reached the straddled metal poles. We lay on the ground underneath them. Standa and the girl dropped down on the ground a bit off to the side, talking non-stop. He sounded like an air compressor running in a neighbouring town beyond him. My ears were glued to him. I was fascinated by his attempts to work his way into the farthest reaches of a girl's soul while on the go. I gaped at the low-sagging lines and the swallows fluttering about them till I got dizzy. I felt as if the ground under our backs had disappeared and we were floating above the land.

'Dude,' the bro turned to me, passing another cigarillo like it was a dove with the olive branch. 'What do you think – is there any point in hooking up with a chick with no boobs?'

'How do you mean, no boobs?' I asked.

'No boobs at all!'

'For sure,' I said after a bit.

We lay there at least another half hour.

'We should be heading back,' said Standa Vanča into the sky and stretched himself out. Then he got up, bent over, picked up a stick and weighed it in his hand. Then he hit himself in the face swiftly and hard with it. A raspberry-red discharge sprang out at once.

'What the hell are you doing?' I jumped up.

'Ssimple,' he responded calmly. 'You went out to fight, right? And firsst, you're a friend and ssecond, thiss guy here can't just come back in disgrace, sso I'm taking it upon mysself and I don't want to talk about it anymore.'

The only one who took it matter-of-factly was the girl. Without a word, she took out a handkerchief, ran to the creek to wet it and started tending to the poet. She was squeezing his short blunt nose which he stuck out in the position of a bag-piper while he continued chattering: 'Then I worked a classic job as a medical orderly and a few blue-collar gigss, I was alsso at alcohol rehab centre a couple of timess. And then I wass invited to take part in an open competition for the job of the warden of the casstle Točník 'causse the current warden'd hanged himself – Wünch was his name – sso they quickly needed a replacement but thiss other guy got the job instead back then, and later he came to ssee me saying: Look, I can ssee you care about this sstuff, I could put in a word for you with the heritage buildingss consservationisstss, they're looking for people, you interested? So I figured why not give it a try, right, and to this day I've travelled to and documented eight hundred churches in Central Bohemia alone, so that's about how things are with me...'

Bro and I silently trailed behind them. Once in front of the restaurant, Bro straightened himself up, and went in first. There was no one sitting inside anymore, though. 'They went to Jirsák's to watch a video,' the bartender informed him. Bro turned on the spot, said 'see ya' and shot out of there leaving us sitting behind. We each had a grog. Standa Vanca with a swollen nose protested when I wanted to buy it for him. Slit-eyes kept looking at him silently and with sadness. The time to leave was fast approaching.

We dawdled towards the train station, and only just made it.

Standa unexpectedly stepped up to me and hugged me saying: 'Well, I'm glad I had a chance to get to know you. That reading wass good, like I ssaid I jusst didn't like that you got nervouss in the process... When ssomeone'ss after your throat, there'ss only one rule: stand up for yourself! But there'ss no doubt you and I will meet again, I jusst don't know when, becausse I've just decided to sstay here with thiss girl.'

Slit-eyes was looking down with a pink smile on her face. She moved her solid, country-girl calves, stuffed in hick jeans, like a prima ballerina.

'And what are you gonna do here?' I asked.

'Drive a truck or somethin', dunno...'

We turned around, each leaving in a different direction, me heading for the platform, which didn't even look very much like one, them going god-knows where, towards houses surrounded by hawthorns reminiscent of Masaryk's time with their branches broken off, and past those houses, farther and away. I looked back a few times. I could tell even from his motionless back that he was still talking at her on and on and on.

★

That afternoon I found myself back home, and I immediately climbed into bed because it was obvious that last night's sojourn outside the sleeping bag wouldn't be without some consequences. I stretched my achy joints, swallowed some flu medicine and simply lay down for a while, thinking about the trip that had just ended. Then I picked up the pile of the bailiff's short stories. Before I managed to read the first sentence, my window onto the street shuddered and I heard an ear-splitting ruckus: *Bzzhsss, chchch... Bang!*

I jumped up and threw a shirt on. *Bzzhsss, chchch... Bang!*

I drew the curtain aside and saw small pieces of smashed ceramic shingles raining hard onto my window sill. Fine, all-pervading dust was rolling over everything. The sides of the container resonated nearby. The only barrier separating my flat from pure hell was the thin, poorly insulated window.

I walked through the hall filling with swirling opaque fog and opened the main entrance door.

*BZZHSSS, CHCHCH... BANG!* Another pile of rubble with broken planks flew down the chute into the metal skip and thickened the air into an unbreathable consistency. There was knocking and hammering and banging coming from above.

I stood there staring, feeling like a cornered and trapped animal. What to do? Should I quickly try getting some insulation or a plastic sheet or some such thing to put around the window? Should I leave everything and take off? Should I turn on the gas, lock the door and try starting from scratch somewhere else? Should I climb into the skip in protest and stay there until removed by the police? To be hauled into a loony-bin? To shout at some poor lady doctor on reception that this is a shitty world? Should I go somewhere covered in dust to complain? All things considered, the idea with the skip was the only one that seemed to make sense to me. It would make a splash if nothing else, and no one could then claim that we were all living here happily ever after.

'You fucking cunts!' I roared up towards the roof.

The knocking stopped. The friendly face of a workman slowly emerged over the eaves.

'Why?'

'Because we live here, damn it!' I shouted. 'Who can live in such mess?'

'It's just for two weeks,' the face replied softly. 'C'mon, you can tough it out, can't you?'

'OK, we'll tough it out,' I nodded and tried closing the old, uninsulated entrance door behind me as best as I could and went back to bed.

# The End of the World

ORIGINALLY I JUST went over on some errands. I rang the doorbell of a fancy door in a comfortable bourgeois apartment building near the embankment – one of those typical buildings where the residents still remember the reprisals after Heydrich's assassination in 1942. The peephole turned dark for a moment, then the door chain rattled.

A thin woman, going on forty, opened the door. She had bags under her eyes and her mouth had been enlarged by lipstick to an unbelievable size. She was wearing a skirt and a completely see-through black blouse with nothing underneath. I tried not to look at her breasts there in the doorway but despite my good intentions I began to address them, 'Hello, I'm...'

The breasts answered in an unexpectedly husky two-toned voice, 'Hi!'

Somehow it all fitted together, so I wasn't particularly surprised. The breasts said, 'Don't take your shoes off, just come in!'

The woman offered me her hand, shook her bracelets and without further ado went to make coffee. She jabbered from the kitchenette non-stop. From what she was telling me, I felt like the last time I saw her was two days ago. She had the incredible ability to talk about several things at the same time.

'Have a seat... you sitting?... Jirka was here, he... looks like that actor... Drtina... he's a bit jealous of me, you know and... I wanted to go to see *Prattling Snail...* but he won't take me there, he says he might bump into... this Machytka

149

guy there, he owes him some money or somethin', I think he played cards with someone and lost, he doesn't tell me everything... you might know him... so these days I just feel, I don't wanna say lonely, but... I was in the National Theatre's ballet for fifteen years, you know... I danced in the corps de ballet, so I was used to having people around, and... I wanted... do you take milk in your coffee?... I wanted to try something on my own, something I'd enjoy, but Ivan... he's all right, I respect him, but he's not reliable and he tends to... I don't wanna say use people, you know, but I keep an eye on him, you wanna see the pictures? Wait, they must be here somewhere...'

Cigarette in hand she started to rummage through the shelves until a big pile of papers, envelopes and letters tumbled down. Pictures from one of the envelopes fell onto the carpet, 'Here they are... so here, see... The Nation to Itself... this is me... just a few years younger...'

There she was in the large, damaged black and white photographs in ballet tights, with a nervous smile, a long narrow nose on her pale face, thin, ten years younger, pretty. And unlike in real life, one thing was apparent, some kind of obvious, irresistible magic; she emanated sweet perfume, make-up, alcohol, sleeping pills, mothballs and vanity.

She laughed, 'Do you like me here... actually... a funny thing to ask, I mean do you feel that... Ivan told me you perform or performed at Dobeška, he also performed at Vašinka's but that was way back, he said that... here, you see we were rehearsing Vest Sajd Story, but it didn't go through in the end, 'cause it was directed by a... he defected to Austria, they almost fired me because of that 'cause you know... you know Marek?...'

'No.'

She pulled an open bottle of vodka from the freezer, 'I see, I thought... last week I went for a walk at Letná, a friend of mine lives there, her brother jumped under a train a month ago, he jumped onto the tracks from a little bridge but he didn't kill himself, he was just unconscious and that's when the motor train ran over him, the engineer didn't notice a thing, and he lay there on the tracks with his legs cut off, they were sliced off right here,' she drew her dark red painted nail across her thin thigh. 'He was still alive for half an hour, by the time they found him the poor man's hair was white, he had turned completely grey in that little while, he died on them in the ambulance, so you can see how she must... they grew up together and this year they found a growth in her breast, and last year, you see, their mother gassed herself to death, so you can... we went... I went for a walk by the Hanavský Pavillion, near Šebesťák's place, have you been there? He's the way he is, I actually quite like him, even though I certainly have a reason to avoid him, which is an old story... you're not drinking at all! Is there something you want?'

'If you had some Tylenol...'

'I mean in life, if there's something... you want?'

Both breasts were casting a mysterious downward look at me from underneath the chiffon, while becoming pointier and pointier.

She gestured towards a shiny, worn leather chair standing in front of the piano. It was black, studded with iron hob-nails on each side, and it was bleak and solid like the easy-chair from the SS villa in the movie *The Higher Principle*. Judging by the dust-bunnies that floated and rolled around the keyboard cover every time one of us spoke a little louder, no one had played the piano in a long time.

'The chair belonged to Nezval, d'you know Nezval, the poet...?'

'Yeah.'

'My parents got it... from his estate. Do you like Nezval?'

How could I not like that Roman-nosed phantom of the Czechoslovak operetta, who would have fed on chocolate cream puffs, Choux Paste, cream horns and pralines no matter the regime! How could I not like that salon bushman, who'd pose in his swimsuit pulled all the way above his navel by the Sázava river; that tearful prince with the body of a mother of four, whose melancholy and conceited self-love eventually brought about the blooming peonies of the *Edison* and *Wondrous Magician* – poems whose fragrance one can smell to this day...!

'So sit on it, if you want...'

'Thanks. I'll stay here...'

Turning into a pussycat, she pouted her lips, 'Why don't you sit there a bit for meee...'

It struck me that perhaps she wanted to get me drunk, tie me to the easy chair so that she could go on telling me whatever came to her mind until I slowly went insane. She'd feed me spaghetti without ketchup and pour *pigi* tea into me to keep me alive for a few days. Or perhaps I reminded her of her deceased father who spent the last fifteen years of his life in that chair.

I sat down in the chair. That same moment, she pulled two bottles of white wine from the fridge: 'I found some Riesling... would you like some?'

Buried in the squeaky leather trap, which had been polished shiny by the poet's fat buttocks, I listened to her rambling, cooing and rattling. For a good hour I didn't hear what she was saying, fascinated by her uneasy facial expressions. Her lips would occasionally form a slow and cynical 's'. Now and then they would conjure up a big 'oh'. Occasionally they would utter 'Yep that's how it is...!' She looked like a girl who'd secretly rummaged through her mother's make-up and defiantly plastered a big red mouth on top of her lips in the hall mirror. She wasn't in control. That made her different from most other women. She looked like a clown and she behaved like one, too. She kept dropping things. Spilled her coffee. Burned a hole in the couch with her cigarette. Burned a hole through the curtain when she was looking out the window. She was a handshake between joy and terror.

The bookcase was full of rolls of paper, boxes, empty bottles, dusty teddy-bears. On one shelf there was a book bound in brown cloth, its title in Cyrillic script read, 'Alisa v Stranye Chudyes.'[28]

It showered lightly outside, and then the weather turned nice and darkness began to fall. Time for a cozy chat in the twilight. I went to take a leak. In the loo, I happened to cast my eyes upon a basket under the sink filled to the brim with used pads. I studied this intriguing phenomenon with detachment. The bottom layers were all shriveled and caked together while the top ones must have been just a few hours old. I thought again of the poet Nezval; and also about the sculptor Gebauer with his unhealthy grey parrots stuffed into wire cages that were too small for them. I returned to the room and sank again into the wing chair. Being in a cobweb might not be all that uncomfortable... depending on the circumstances. And circumstances are fortunately almost always clear only in hindsight.

I dropped by a bar to buy her cigarettes. When I came back she was finishing up the wine. 'I... wanna go to bed... if you want... you can stay here... I mean if... well, it's up to you...'

I hastily brushed my teeth with a frayed toothbrush and this time tried not to look at the basket under the sink.

She lay on an open sofa bed in her nightie. Under the nightie her ballet legs were nicely folded with her thin ankles encircled by clear blue aristocratic veins. I lay beside her. I pulled the blanket over myself. Under the blanket we grabbed each other and that was that.

At one point I realized that the whole room had turned a hundred and eighty degrees. I didn't know how I'd achieved it but I felt like a death rider turning in the middle of a sweet cloud of burnt petrol, in a wire globe in the middle of an arena. To my amazement, I realized that I

28. Alice in Wonderland.

was leaning with my feet against the bookcase in a handstand while she was nicely hooked up into me crosswise, moving fast, fast, the sweat pouring out of our bodies like water and her cracked voice rattling up close into my ear, 'It's nice... like this... isn't it...'

We were doing rolls of sorts, turning summersaults of sorts and flips... I could see that she was indeed a ballerina. She had danced half her life away in the National Theatre, while I had drunk it away in bars. Her thin trained body had its own idea about what it wanted, it had a mind of its own. To tell you the truth, a couple of hours later I fainted... She brought me back to life a few more times and everything started from scratch. It started to rain again. Moths flew into the room through the open window to save themselves from drowning.

The sun was shining again in the morning. With great exertion I opened my peepers. Her head lay on a pillow beside me, watching me. Cutting straight to the chase, she said, 'Please... don't say anything...'

I went into the bathroom and put my head under the cold shower. It helped for a bit.

I was so mixed-up that I wrote down my phone number for her without being asked. Then I went to work four hours late.

About two weeks later Karel Bursík, who relieved me at work, told me, 'Hans, you got a call from some writer or something... she spent half an hour telling me about some... well... she wants you to call her at this number...'

He said it while disapprovingly peering out the window. He uttered the word 'writer' in a way that didn't make me want to ask anything more. I felt branded with shame but didn't know what for. After he left I put water on for coffee, fed and scratched the two cats that were milling about my feet and dialed the number. I could hear the crackling from Podolí: 'Hi, I called you at work but you weren't there, so I... But instead there was some... very nice man, we had a really good chat...'

'What about?'

'That's a secret... About you, among other things... if you like, I'll fill you in on it when you come and visit me... I mean if you want... to come and visit me...'

I knew that I shouldn't go there, which is precisely why I knew I would in the end.

I walked along the embankment and thought of dozens of things I would rather be doing that very moment. In the middle of my thoughts I entered her building. A terribly fat woman was toiling up the stairs, resting every three steps and gasping for breath, and she managed it just so that she could see the door I'd stopped in front of, wiped the sweat off her forehead and shot at me, 'Looking for someone?'

I rang the doorbell. A pale little face with lipstick like a squished carnation appeared in the gap as the door opened. 'Hi.'

In the hall I was engulfed in a cloud of perfume. She was wearing a peculiar denim coat that went down to her feet and had at least twenty five large carefully closed red buttons. She looked like a vivandière. 'That's Stoklasová... a nosy bitch... You'll have some coffee, right... I've had four already... but I'll have one with you... Jirka was here, you know... so I'm a bit nervous but please ignore that... I was gonna ask you if you'd be into taking a steamboat trip up to the Slapy dam on Saturday, some of my former colleagues will be there, but you don't need to worry... Brigita would love to meet you... I think it will be... nice... I just hope that the Machytka guy won't show up, I hear he... wants the money from me...'

I went straight to the black chair without waiting to be asked. We chatted for a while. Then she expressed a wish to go for a walk with me.

The pavements were virtually deserted. She was clicking beside me like a geisha, still wearing the jacket buttoned all the way down, with her bare feet in half-crazy bright red shoes. I thought the only place we could go like this, without attracting too much attention, would be the Matejská Fair... We'd surely look great, me and her, on the chair swing. She locked her arm into mine. I was wearing an old worn-out leather jacket. It originally had overstuffed shoulder padding so I had cut a few large strips of foam from the places I was able to reach. I went on to wear the jacket for ten years without being able to admit to myself that there were terribly shriveled superfluous bags hanging from my shoulders. Now I could see it in a shop window as we crossed a street: her big mouth that never stopped chattering, and beside her someone wearing a stiff smile, nodding and obligingly holding out his rigid sleeve like that of an insect, and her hanging on to it with both hands.

We looked like characters from a Hungarian movie. As if the two of us were quietly trying to sort out some Budapest problems of ours. In this way we walked all the way to the botanical garden. The gate was open. We went in. It was deserted. Dry palm-trees were swaying in wooden planters. Galingales were crackling. Rhododendrons were blooming.

She leaned against the trunk of a yellow poplar. 'You wanna... see something?'

I looked at her and saw that whatever happened now would have the significance of a premeditated plan. I nodded. She undid a button at her neck, then another one, and another. She undid all twenty five. Her eyes became peaceful. There was nothing but the reflection of the silent pit of the blue sky. She wore nothing under her coat. I saw everything that had gone unnoticed before. She must have weighed about forty kilos. Her two breasts stuck out above her pitiful dog-like ribs, screaming for help. Her stomach was lined with a tangle of deep scars – it looked as if it had been cut up and then stitched back together. From below her girly protruding pelvis furiously, there peered a spooky hairy bugaboo. It looked as if it was about to speak. I instinctively turned off my brain because whatever might come from it would hurt her. I did the only thing that was left for me to do: I opened my pants and, right then and there, in a more or less open space, began to bang her. She spread her legs as if she wanted to fly away. She hooked herself into me without a word, tears streaming down her face. I was wiping them and smearing about her face some purple shit she'd used to paint it.

Not far away stood a guy in a checkered shirt staring right at us. There was no expression worth mentioning on his face. He just stood there, stared, and kept silent. All I could do was ignore him.

She cut her nails into my back creating ten deep gashes from which my lazy city-boy blood began to stream down my pants. An unlikely fragrance emanated from the yellow poplar's blossoms. I kissed her repeatedly not knowing how else to pacify her, yet feeling that by doing so I was breaking through the last thin door to her desperation, which was the last thing I wanted. Wads of cotton wool went through my mind. Large sheets of meaningless bullshit billowed out as far as the eye could see. The city was squeaking, swaying and floating on the face of the Earth, on and on. Nobody really knew why they were living. In the pubs, shots of hard liquor shone and tacky jokes sparkled around. Red-hot fireballs, which shone and quickly burnt out, were continuously dashing above a cooling mash of the human spirit. Men tortured women with their inexplicable silence. Women tortured men with irrational reproaches. Children in kindergarten already knew how to make each other's lives most miserable. Nobody had the faintest idea what awaited them the next day. They were all afraid to think about it, yet they all had to think about it. That created a peculiar surface tension; it was the best thing of all. They were all certain this could not yet be the end of the world, because this was not what the end of the world looked like. They knew from the movies what it might look like. Some had an inkling that with a bit of fantasy it could all come about differently... but even they were wrong. Everybody was still missing the most fundamental fact, which is that the world cannot possibly end for everybody at once; just for each person individually. Because reality is nothing but a combination of wishes and hopes. The end of the world is an entirely personal category. What seems like the end of the world to one, might, to another, be a reason to open a bottle to celebrate the real thing.

The guy in the checkered shirt was still standing there. He didn't move an inch. I didn't care. I kneeled and buried my nose into the living bugaboo. On and on I licked her silent weeping cunt and felt like melting into the sadness, the mess, the eternity, the ever-revolving-all-crushing combine-harvester of expectations and disappointments; but I couldn't. I was no Hyperion. I lost any courage.

I stood in the botanical garden in the middle of the day embracing a sobbing, naked forty year-old woman. I was thirty two. Large leaves of strange trees and bushes rustled in the wind.

The guy in the shirt had disappeared.

I buttoned up her jacket. I gave her a handkerchief to wipe the smudges off her face. I had no idea that my own mug looked like that of a baboon, thanks to her lipstick.

I left her standing there. With confusion in my soul, I went out onto the street full of idiots like me. I felt better among them. They were the only ones with whom I had anything at all to talk about.

# About the Author

**Emil Hakl** (aka Jan Beneš) was born in Prague in 1958. After graduating from the Jaroslav Jezek Conservatorium, he worked as a copywriter and as the editor of the literary magazine *Tvar*. In the late 80s, Hakl founded an informal literary group called Moderní Analfabet. Hakl made his literary debut with two collections of poetry, followed shortly by a collection of stories *Konec sveta* [*The End of the World*] (2001). Since then Hakl has written a novel, *Intimní schránka Sabriny Black* [Sabrina Black's Intimate Box] (2002), a novella, *O rodicích a detech* [On Kids and Parents] (2002), and a second collection of stories, *O létajících objektech* [On Flying Objects] (2004). *O rodicích a detech* (2002) won the distinguished Magnesia Litera Prize and has been adapted into a feature film by Vladimír Michálek.

## About the Translators

**Petr Kopet**, originally from Prague, studied English and Linguistics at Simon Fraser University in Canada, where he makes his home. His translations from English include John Lennon's *In His Own Write*, Douglas Adams' *The Meaning of Liff*, Alex Ross' *The Rest is Noise* and translations from Czech include Jan Neruda's *Malá Strana Stories* and short stories by *Emil Hakl*.

**Karen Reppin** lives in Vancouver, where she teaches ESL at Douglas College. She served as the President of the British Columbia branch of the Editors' Association of Canada for several years. She also translates from German to English, and her translations include Franz Kafka's *The Metamorphosis*, *The Letter to Father*, and Harald Salfellner's *Franz Kafka and Prague*.

## Special Thanks

The publishers would like to thank Antonia Lloyd-Jones and Andrea Rozic for their help in translating the Polish and Croatian excerpts, respectively. Thanks are also due to Tom Roselle, Harriet Whitehead and Rosemary Wilkinson for their editorial assistance throughout.

# I Love You When I'm Drunk

## Empar Moliner

### Translated from the Catalan by Peter Bush

978 1905583058
£7.95

Fast, precise, hilariously timed and mercilessly honest, the stories of Empar Moliner lay bare every pretension ever to have offered comfort to the middle class psyche. From the zeal of a mothers' group staging a world record breastfeeding attempt to couples role-playing their way into parenthood at a third world 'adoption workshop', every well-meaning fad and right-on gesture is brilliantly observed and astutely exposed.

'Deft and ingenious'
— *Times Literary Supplement*

'With a fresh and direct language and great humour, Moliner takes the logic of small, everyday situations to their limit'
— *Lift Stuttgart*

www.commapress.co.uk